FURY'S CHILDREN

A Novel of
Psychological Suspense

by
Seymour Shubin

A Write Way Publishing Book

This is a work of fiction. Names, characters, locales and incidents are either the product of the author's imagination or are used fictitiously, and any resemblance to actual persons, living or dead, is entirely coincidental.

Write Way Publishing
10555 E. Dartmouth, Ste 210
Aurora, CO   80014

First Edition; 1997

ISBN 1-885173-35-0

1 2 3 4 5 6 7 8 9

For Gloria
with love

Other Novels by Seymour Shubin

Anyone's My Name
Manta
Wellville, U.S.A.
The Captain
Holy Secrets
Voices
Never Quite Dead
Remember Me Always

CHAPTER ONE

The manager looked over at her from his office, thinking for maybe the fiftieth time in the two months she'd been here the biggest compliment he could think of for a female: she could have been a model, she could have been a doctor's wife.

It was strange, he realized, how he was thinking of her in the past tense when she was only what? Nineteen. But that's the way he thought of her. He saw the slimeball she was going with, and if she married him—and if it wasn't him, it was going to be someone like him—there'd be a lot of kids and a million beers in the refrigerator, and if she didn't grow fat and ugly she'd be thin and ugly. If only someone would teach her you didn't have to have your hair way out to here—it was a honey-colored mop, only wilder—or always have on the brightest red lipstick, and jeans so tight she couldn't be seen to be breathing (and almost always with the highest heels).

And the thing was, she was smart. *Smart*. He'd hired her to stock shelves, then in an emergency tried her out on one of the registers, then in another emergency put her behind the information desk where in no time she rarely had to check the stock list, knew which of the eight long aisles to send people to.

But he was going to have to get rid of her. He'd told

himself that before, only it was for a different reason then, which had been because she never wore the little blue linen company jacket, with the Wilson Home Products logo on the upper pocket, which she still hardly wore even after the warning. And it wasn't only because he couldn't get his eyes off that ass and those tits, but that she kept slipping into his head at home, even last night with Marsha whispering (so the kids wouldn't hear) against his shoulder that she wanted to make love.

He shifted his eyes quickly to some papers beneath his hands, seeing a slight turning of her head.

Terri had caught him, though she looked away fast, not wanting the creep (he was no more than in his early thirties, though he reminded her of someone sixty; he always wore a jacket and *tie* in this place) to think he was *worth* thinking about, even in disgust. She hated him, she hated everyone today, she hated everyone yesterday and the day before—

"Where's the fire extinguishers, miss?"

"Aisle seven, on the left."

"Do you have brackets for the wall, you know, the kind you ..?"

And returns, there were a million returns today; she had to fill out slips, take the crap back, put it under the counter or if it was too heavy call someone over. And she was doing it, doing everything, though her head felt like it was filled with cotton, a beating kind of cotton.

She kept glancing at her watch.

Once, as it was approaching five, she couldn't fight off the impulse and took a partly ripped picture from her handbag she'd torn out of a newspaper. It showed a man of about fifty-five, with gray hair and wearing a V-neck sweater and shorts, smiling as he held a tennis racket across his waist.

Then she put it back quickly. The creep wasn't back there in his office anymore, but she was suddenly aware that someone else might see.

Terri's mother, at the kitchen sink in her brick-and-frame twin in Dowlyn, a community about ten miles outside Philadelphia, had one quick, sinking reaction as she heard the key in the front door: she wished Terri would move out.

It made her feel guilty, for God knows she loved her, but still she wished it.

She heard the door open and close, then the creaking of the steps to the second floor. She couldn't remember the last time Terri'd come home and looked in the living room, the kitchen, to say hello to them before going up. And there was no telling when she'd come down and eat with them—you weren't even allowed to call up to her and ask.

Everyone said, and it was true, that once they leave home they shouldn't come back. This was Terri's third job since high school—the one before this was over in Jersey, and she'd had a place there. But then her car went and then the job, and she came back, asking would they mind if she stayed here until she saved up some money; she'd pay a little, whatever she could.

Actually, Terri's mother hadn't wanted her to leave in the first place; it hadn't seemed right for a girl not yet nineteen, but once she'd gone everything'd settled down in the house. It was as though a giant vacuum sweeper had sucked the arguments, the tensions, out of all the rooms.

The thing was, she was such a beautiful girl and she could be so sweet, though it was harder and harder to remember the times; it was like remembering bits of sunshine during weeks of clouds. All the teachers who'd said she should be getting better marks, she's bright. All the calls from school—"Terri's not here, is she home?" And the boys, all the boys.

She looked toward the staircase now, hearing someone coming down. But it was her husband, Jack. She'd known his walk, but she'd looked a quick, hopeful look anyway.

Terri spread open the blue-and-yellow flowered curtains of her bedroom window and looked down at the street, then toward the corner, as if somehow that would bring Denny here faster. She wouldn't have come home to wait for him—her bus stopped at every corner—if he hadn't said he had to work until six, six-thirty. "Geez, I *can't*," he'd insisted in a frantic little voice, as though his boss was standing right over him.

It was probably too late now, anyway.

But she hated thinking that. She hadn't really put her mind on this until this afternoon, and now there was no shaking it off. She started to leave, thought it over, then went back to her closet, slipped off her shoes and exchanged heels for sneaks. This might not be a time for heels.

Downstairs, her parents looked at her from the living room as she opened the refrigerator. She took the half hoagie she'd saved from yesterday.

"You sure you don't want some meat loaf?" her mother asked.

"No, it's okay."

Her mother kept looking at her; her father looked at her briefly from his reclining chair, then picked up a newspaper.

He was dark-complexioned, with graying black hair, her mother bony, with salt-and-pepper hair, her face weathered by time but still pretty. They'd both been thirty-eight when she was born, eight years after her brother, twelve after her sister ...

She couldn't wait to get outside, to wait there.

And *look*. With all his anger, with all his what-he-was-going-to-do-to-them, with all that, her father was still wearing their T-shirt—NCI. Their *T-shirt*!

***

Denny finished the last lube job. No more than a fifteen minute wait, their ads said, with a dollar off for every minute over. He scrubbed his hands under the faucet and watched for a few lingering moments the grease and dirt drain into the dark-coated sink. Then he went out to his car, a black 1986 Mustang.

He drove fast, not caring that if he was picked up for speeding and they *looked*, they'd find a gun in the glove compartment. That gun was his safety the way the streets were these days.

*C*HAPTER TWO

She waited at the top of the steps, in the light of the small brass fixture over the door, looking toward the corner he would turn to come onto her street. Her beige down jacket was unzipped, for it was fairly warm for February. But the night had the smell of a wood fire, probably the Connors' across the street. A cigarette glowed down in her right hand. She'd taken only one puff in the foyer before stepping out.

Her parents wouldn't miss not seeing Denny.

She walked down the three steps to the sidewalk, as though this too would bring him faster. But she wasn't in the hurry she was before. Something had calmed in her. The whole thing, she'd agreed in herself, was crazy and she should look on it as fun. Something to do, with Denny.

Still, that wasn't quite true, she knew.

A car's lights approached from two blocks away, then curved in front of the Gionelli's, three houses up, and went dark. Mrs. Gionelli lifted out a couple of packages and closed the door with her elbow. The Gionellis had lived here forever, which meant as long as Terri could remember, and she'd been born here. Lots of the families lived here forever, and the new ones who moved in seemed to look like those who moved out.

St. Francis Elementary was five blocks away, her high school, Morgan, about a mile or two. Her parents had done things in reverse—they'd put her in public high to get her away from her friends in parochial. But she'd still kept seeing some of the old kids and met a lot of even livelier ones. Girls, mostly; but then there was Greg, who must have been worth a novena to her parents, for he'd moved away; and then afterward Denny, who would have graduated with her if he hadn't dropped out after his parents' divorce. He was smart, though, knew an awful lot of things. She knew for a fact that he read at least two newspapers a day.

Here he was now.

Someone told her once he looked like James Dean. She'd never seen it until then, but it was true, though Denny's hair was darker and a lot longer. And he had that little hunch of his shoulders when he walked, and especially when he smoked.

He lowered the window and looked up at her, waiting for her to go around to the passenger side.

"Move over," she said, "I want to drive."

"Why?"

"Move over. I know the way."

Terri remembered it, even though the place was way out on the Main Line, near Paoli, and she'd been maybe seven when her father drove them out here and parked across the road where she was parked now; he'd pointed up to the mansion and said, "That's where he lives, that's where Mr. Wyndan"—though she didn't know the spelling of his name then—"lives."

Wyndan had a midget-size train up there—her father had told them about it a hundred times over the years—that went all around the grounds, with crossings and even a station back near where he kept his three or four horses. She used to fantasize being friends with his children and sitting with them on top of the little cars as it went around—it had five cars, her father said, one for each passenger and one for whoever was engineer.

Mike—her brother was about sixteen then, her sister was already married—wanted to know if they could go up the drive and look at it, but her father looked at him as if he was crazy. He took great pride in having been on it himself; he had come here for some reason with one of the men at the plant who'd had to do some repairs at the house. He used to talk about it with pride in his voice that probably wouldn't have even been there if he *owned* the train, the whole house.

And everything was "we."

We got this order from France, we're big up in Mars, we did this, we did that. And all he was, though she couldn't remember having any of these feelings then, was someone who worked in dyes; he always came home with little splatters of colors on him, and there was a line of black under his nails that he'd had for as far back as she could remember.

Asshole.

Even when the rumors started almost a year ago that a lot of people would be going, "naah," he wouldn't be one of them. At least that's what her mother used to tell her for him, for she and her father rarely talked anymore, since just about every time they did there'd be some argument. But then it began changing, he began worrying—she'd never seen him drink a pack of beer in her life; and when he did go, and the boss still making a billion a year, he was going to get himself a gun, oh, was he going to get himself a gun, was he going to do this, that; then he began settling into he was going to get together with people and sue. And then, not even that. The air went out of him.

"What do you think? What do you want to do?"

That again? All the way here that's all Denny'd been saying. And he knew everything she knew. She didn't know what she wanted to do. The paper said Wyndan was getting an award tonight—something about indoor tennis, country club indoor tennis—and there he was smiling in the picture, and all she knew was she'd never hated a face more. And she'd come here thinking everyone might be away at the awards, that the house would give off enough of a look of emptiness in the night that she could hurt him by at least hurting something he owned. Like the train. Or the greenhouse that was somewhere back there. But now that she was here that was total shit, something she'd known well enough all along but not the way she knew it now. And anyway the house and grounds were brightly lit, and there must be three cars up there on the circular drive.

"What do you say?" Denny was saying.

She had to come down. She was still on a high, but the turn had come on it; it was a depressing high now.

"I'd like to do something, you know that," he said. "But this—I mean, just sit."

He was right, that was part of it being crazy. This was like a country road. She'd kept the motor on idle, to get some heat, but the lights were out. She turned them on now and, still looking up there, slowly pulled away.

He said, "You eat anything? I didn't eat anything."

She was looking where to make a U-turn now.

"These sonsabitches, they really live," Denny said, looking around. "Goddamn houses are like forty miles apart."

She missed the first driveway to turn around on, but did it on the second. As they headed back, she saw headlights fan out from the Wyndan's drive, then a car turned onto the road in the direction she was going. She stepped just a little harder on the gas, enough to get a bit closer.

"That's no limo," Denny said. "You'd think if it's one of them, it'd be a limo."

She wished he'd shut up.

"But these wealthies, they got shit cars, too," he said. "You oughta see some I see. I see a shit car, the guy doesn't even want a new filter, some of 'em don't even want a new *fan* belt, and you ought to see some of the fancy addresses. Gladwyne. Devon."

They were turning onto a somewhat trafficked street now. Terri drew closer.

Denny said, leaning toward the windshield, his head turned slightly as though he were focusing a telescope, "It's a Lincoln Town Car." He shrugged noncommittally.

After about a mile, she tried to pull out alongside it but couldn't because of a car passing her.

"What you trying to do?" he asked.

"See who's in there."

She was able to go around now. She pulled next to the Lincoln, but far enough off not to have heads turn. The windows weren't the dark kind, but it was still hard to see in. A man was driving and there was no one next to him. Though she concentrated on him, a quick glance revealed there was no one in the back seat, either.

She let up on the gas and drifted back and then behind. Nodding quickly: "Him. It's him. I'm sure."

"You'd think he'd have a chauffeur." Then, soon, "What are we doing?" There was an edge of tension in his voice.

"Just driving," she said. "I just want to see."

"Look, I'm with you, babe," he said quickly, thinking maybe she'd taken it wrong.

He put his hand on her thigh. She barely knew it was there, and after about a half minute he lifted it away. He leaned forward, his hands one big fist on his lap.

The Lincoln was making another turn now, then soon another. After two or three miles it slowed up and pulled into a drive and then stopped briefly between two stone pillars before moving on. She drove by slowly. A bronze tablet on one of the pillars said APPLETON COUNTRY CLUB. A security guard stood on one side of the entrance.

She pulled alongside a darkened service station.

It was as though a gate had clanked down in front of her.

They came back to Dowlyn to Turner's, a luncheonette a few blocks from her home named after the street it was on, not the owner. It was owned by a Lebanese and his wife, whom all the kids knew as Tash and Sonia; if Terri had ever heard their last name, she'd forgotten it long ago. The luncheonette had a long counter on one side, some red vinyl-covered booths on the other, a glass-door refrigerator filled with bottled beer in the front, and a few arcade games in back. It was popular with the kids even though no one ever knew Tash or Sonia to sell beer to a kid or let anyone stay who smelled of grass.

If you wanted to drink beer or smoke grass, one of the places you used to go was down in the park at night, near the creek. But that became too hot—you never knew when the flashlights would come. But the bust the cops liked best, the kids used to joke, was for screwing. It wasn't just out of fear of cops, but she never once let anyone touch her in the park.

She hadn't smoked grass in maybe a year. She'd never been that big on it, then lost all taste for it. And she'd only tried coke twice, three years ago, when she was going out with Greg and he got wound up with the Wildboys, the bikers who were here about six months until the cops pushed them on. That had been an exciting time. And she still remembered when Tony, in his shiny-black German helmet, looked at her over his shoulder, tapped the back seat of his big Harley, questioned her with his eyes, then gave her a grin and roared off.

It had been tempting, though.

Greg thought she'd made it with Tony, which ended up in a big fight and she didn't see him for two or three weeks. She never made it with one boy when she was making it with another, and she was almost always going steady. And there'd only been three of them, though it had started early, when she was thirteen. But she knew of girls who did it way earlier.

Denny said, standing over her as she sat down at a booth, "What do you want?"

He'd taken off his black leather jacket, and had on only a white T-shirt, which she hated, maybe because it reminded her of her father. Most guys she knew who wore T-shirts in the winter had tattoos. But like her father, Denny didn't have a tattoo. He looked nice in those Levis though, even though these were grease-stained. And those cowboy boots, which he almost always wore. She had almost the exact kind, though she wore them outside her jeans.

She was looking around, trying to decide. Then she shook her head. "Nothing."

"Nothin'?"

She looked again, mostly because Sonia, whom she hadn't seen in a couple of months, had just now looked at her with a smile from behind the counter.

"How you doin', sweetie?"

"Good, Sonia. You?" She was a round-faced woman whom Terri had never seen without an apron.

"Oh." She lifted her palms, then went back to one of the three men at the counter. There weren't any kids in the place right now.

Terri said, looking at Denny, "Get me a Coke. And one of those pretzels." A few large soft pretzels lay under a plastic lid on the counter.

"They gotta be hard this time of night."

"Just get it, will you? And put on mustard."

She felt a little beating on both sides of her throat. It had been a strain to say even a few words to Sonia.

For the past few moments she'd been driving behind Wyndan's car again. And then somehow the car was stopped and he was facing her, maybe out in a woods like, and his hands were raised at her gun and the pee was spreading out in his pants. Just that. Or they took his clothes away and beat it. Or, and this was the one that lasted a little longer, she had Denny go up to him and hit him until he was all bloody.

Do you have to do everything you think? the nun had asked.

It wasn't too strange she was remembering that; she thought of that time once in a while. Maybe because it had been such a shock. It was at St. Francis; she was in the seventh grade. She'd played hooky two days straight, then was made to stay home, and then when she came back she had to see this nun she'd never seen before. And she had to look at drawings and blobs of stuff, then the nun asked her a million questions. What do you think of this, that, your mother, father, sister, brother? And then that one question: *Do you feel*—that was the word, feel—*you have to do everything you think?*

There'd been a lot of other questions, but somehow that's the one that stuck in her mind, though she didn't remember her answer.

All she remembered, mostly, was the shock of having to see this nun and answer all those questions. Like if she didn't answer them right she'd have to go to a home. But not only didn't she have to go to a home, no one, not a nun, not her mother and father, ever mentioned it again. It was like it never happened.

She wished she had it to answer today: You don't do *everything*, but you do *some* things.

*C*HAPTER THREE

Denny brought over her Coke and pretzel before going back for his grilled steak and onions sandwich on an Italian roll. Denny opened a fresh pack of Marlboro regulars, and tapped one out for her and then for himself, lighting them with his Bic. Denny still smoked some grass.

"Pretty dead here," he said.

It was. The three men had left, a few people had come in for takeout beer, and the only sound was a distant pinging and thumping from in back, where two kids had come in to play the games. They were high school kids she only knew by sight. She and Molly and Patty and Joanie used to come here at least once a day, and if not in here outside. Tash and Sonia never let more than five or six kids hang out outside at one time. But that seemed so far back in the past, though it was only about a year. And it wasn't only this place, it was other things. It was maybe eight months since she'd been to a rock concert—she always used to be at the Tower Theater over in Upper Darby, or the Spectrum in Philly. She rarely even played her disc player anymore—the last time was a week ago; she'd bought a Metallica album, which didn't do all that much for her. And she'd even brought home only one of her posters for her room, an old Kiss. It was like gauze had come over her life.

The girls, even the girls—she never saw Molly anymore. Molly was married and her husband was going to trade school and his parents let her take over their card shop. She hardly ever saw Patty either, who was also married and pregnant; and except for exchanging a couple of calls she barely ever even talked to Joanie, who was going to community college, was hoping to be a nurse. The only one of the girls she'd seen lately hadn't really been a friend anyway. Miss Prissy, who always tried to hang around with them. She had an ass so tight in school she probably couldn't get a Q-tip in it. But there she was outside her old house, waiting for a taxi to 30th Street Station. She was living in New York now, and out it came, she was an escort. And more—that she never let herself come, would make believe all the time that she was somewhere else, how she traveled all around, several times like to Florida when a guy went there on vacation with his family and he'd put her up at this other hotel. And even about her period, how she'd put something up there so the guy would never know.

Miss Prissy! She could screw a garbage truck for all Terri cared; but *don't* tell it to *me*, it tells me what you think of *me*.

The one most single worst thing she'd ever done was get picked up and taken to the station for speeding when she didn't have a license, and it was as though the cops had been waiting for her for years.

She squeezed out her cigarette as Denny was closing in on the end of his sandwich. She tried to hurry him with her eyes. She felt jumpy, had to get out of here.

"Man," he said when they were finally out, "can't I drive my own car?" But he said it good-humoredly, in fact almost as if he was proud of her. She'd gotten right behind the wheel and he was standing looking down at her, his arm crooked across the top of the door. Then he came around and slid in next to her.

"Got cold," he said, rubbing his hands. "Give us some heat."

She didn't move, sat holding the key.

"Let's go to my condo," he said. It was a room above a flower shop.

She shook her head, still thinking. She felt his arm go around her, his lips touch her cheek. She turned her head away. "Don't. Not now."

His free hand went to her other cheek, then slid down to her left breast. "Don't!" she flared, whirling.

"What's the matter, what's the matter?" he asked, sitting back. Christ—you could almost see him thinking it—they'd screwed three times just yesterday.

"I asked you don't!"

"All right, all right."

She looked at him, then took a deep breath as though that would push away anything that filled her mind. But it didn't, and her hand went briefly to his thigh, just long enough to squeeze it, then she turned on the ignition. The squeeze took the hurt and anger out of him, and he looked on curiously, sometimes with a little smile, as she drove. He didn't say anything until he saw the direction she was going.

"No," he said, the kind of long no that expressed wonder and even a kind of admiration.

"Scare the shit out of him," she said, as though to herself. "Even ... make him take a wrong turn."

"Baby, baby," he said, shaking his head, smiling.

He lit a cigarette, offered it to her. She shook her head and he pulled in deep. Once in a while, staring ahead, he would smile and let out a tiny "ah" to whatever he was thinking. The only time he spoke was when they got closer, and he said, "A left there," though she knew it.

There was no guard at the entrance to the Appleton Country Club and she drove in, down a long drive, to a sign that said PARKING, and she followed the arrow and saw that the lot was still filled with cars. She'd just wanted to be sure, and she drove out and, after giving it thought, turned into the first street. She made a U-turn there and parked at the curb by the intersection, the motor on. If he went home the way he came he would have to come by here. The problem was it would be jammed with cars and she could only hope there wouldn't be too many black Lincoln Town Cars that had an X and R on the plate. And that she could cut in close enough behind it.

She did take a cigarette this time.

They couldn't see the entrance from here; the only way they would be able to tell was with the first change in the traffic, which was almost nothing now.

It started about a half hour later, the approaching hum of motors and then the first cars. Releasing the handbrake quickly, she edged even closer to the intersection. She'd deliberately picked a street without a traffic light, but that made problems too, for the cars, at least the first ones, were going by fast. It was like speed-reading them. But now the traffic was slowing up, thickening.

Denny said, even as she saw it, "There."

Only he said "I think" after it, by which time, even though she wasn't absolutely sure either, she cut the first little part of the car into the first little opening. There was a loud, long honking, but she was through. The Lincoln had to be at least four cars in front and over on the other lane. There was nothing to do but stay back and hope.

The cars were thinning out. She cut over to the other lane, but there were still a couple of cars between her and the Lincoln. And now the Lincoln was making a left at a green light. The cars in front were starting to slow up, as though they were living for red, but they were going through it now. She made the turn fast. The Lincoln was about a half block away, with nothing behind it. She sped up—X and R!—then slowed before she got too close.

She followed for almost twenty minutes. A car pulled in front of her once, and she was about to cut around it, but then it passed the Lincoln, too. The street was just about empty. They were out in the suburbs, but it was still pretty far from where he lived. The Lincoln slowed up, then stopped for a red light.

She'd slowed with it, was about twenty yards in back, slowed even more—and then suddenly, as if something had burst open in her head, she began gently pressing and giving up on the brake, then inched into the Lincoln's bumper. Denny said, "Jesus," then saw where her hand was going, grabbed it before it got to the glove compartment. But she tore free, opened it, grabbed the gun. His hand covered hers, was tearing at her fingers for the gun, now had it.

"Do it!" she cried. "Do it, do him!"

His eyes were wide, his mouth open, his face chalk-white. He sat frozen, staring at her. He wasn't going to do it! All he'd done was take the gun from her. She tore at the gun again and he pulled it away, dazed.

"Then *you* do it, do it, do it!"

The driver was maneuvering himself out of the Lincoln. He started to look at the rear, then at them.

"Den!"

His eyes went from her to the driver. And now he was out of the car. He walked right up to him, fired twice, then seemed to just hang there as the man fell. Then Den started to bend over him.

But now a woman was standing by the passenger side, was screaming, her hands to her head; she kept screaming as Denny ran, bent over, back to the car.

She cut in and out of streets, once turning off her lights

before realizing that was worse. And that going fast was worse. Slow. Go normal.

"Why'd we do it?" Denny moaned. "I never thought we'd really *do* it."

"Why the hell did you stay there?" she screamed. "What were you bendin' over him for? Tryin' to steal something?"

"No—I don't know—I thought maybe see if he was still alive. I don't know. Why'd we do it?" And then when he got no answer, "Where you goin' now? What're we doin'?"

"The gun"—her voice was lower now, firm—"have to get rid of the gun."

Not in a sewer, she knew the cops searched sewers. No trash can. No woods, someone always found it in the woods. The river? They always seemed to get them up from the river, too.

She had to stop somewhere, she was breathing too hard. She pulled into an alley. He said, "What're we doin'?" and his breath was going hard, too. She didn't answer; she didn't really know.

They began looking again where to get rid of the gun. But it was as though the world with all its gullies, caves, forests, rivers, had become smooth as glass. He pointed out what must have been two dozen places, but nothing was safe enough for her. Until she realized what she wanted.

Everything was changed now, she wanted it somewhere in the house where she could get to it fast. Or even right here in her handbag.

It was almost three when she let Denny drive her home. He wanted her to stay at his place; he seemed fine now and she wanted to go home. She hated it there, but something was drawing her back.

She was amazed how calm she was.

She unlocked the door and closed it quietly behind her,

turning off the outside light. There was also a light on in the living room. She thought he might be up, smoking one of his million cigarettes, his body, which used to be so big to her and maybe it was then, shrunken and hollow-chested in his NCI T-shirt. But they had left the light on for her.

She started to go into her room, paused, then went back to theirs. The door was open. She couldn't remember how long ago her parents had begun sleeping with the door open. They were sleeping back to back in a sprawl of blankets.

She looked at her father.

She wished she could tell him. She wanted to yell it at him: *I did what you couldn't do!*

*C*HAPTER FOUR

Within moments after the two pops of the gun and the woman's first scream, the surrounding houses came alive with lights; doors opened, people stepped out hesitantly, then some ran out to the street. She was on her knees over him, moaning now, rocking back and forth. Blood flowed from where his right eye had been and slowly spread over his clothes from his chest.

The first police car got there in minutes, and now other sirens were converging. Television vans, three of them, began pulling up. The night seemed colder with the figure on the ground, especially under flashlights and now floodlights. There was no great rush anymore; whoever had reason to would kneel next to the body and then abandon it. Most of the cops seemed to be just hanging around, though several were talking to knots of neighbors, and others had fanned out to other streets. One was bending next to the open door of the Lincoln, on the passenger side, where the dead man's wife had let herself be led.

But all she was able to tell him was that the killer was trying to rob her husband when she came out. She hadn't seen his face, and all she knew of his car was that it was black.

The only thing the cops knew was that this was a biggie.

There are lives and then there are lives. This was Charles Wyndan, chairman and chief executive officer of North Chemical Industries; socialite, philanthropist, you name the civic organization, the committee, he was probably a member.

But as the cop, a township detective named Zinn, said to a buddy when he came back from the car, "You think you have to be smart to be rich?"

"I know it's dumb to be poor."

Zinn was thinking: how many times before people caught on? After all the stories of people being rear-ended and getting out and being abducted or killed, you'd think they would follow advice and at least drive someplace bright where there were people.

That was one lucky lady; her screaming scared him off.

Rick Broder heard it on the radio in the morning, the little radio on the room divider between his living room and the small kitchen, which had been tuned softly to public broadcasting. He'd just come from the shower, barefoot and in a terrycloth robe, his slightly graying, brownish-red hair still dripping a little water, to sit with coffee and the *New York Times*, when he heard Wyndan's name. And then "killed," "murdered."

Son-of-a-bitch. Charles Wyndan.

He turned to face the radio, listened intently. An award for tennis. Driving with his wife. Rear-ended. "Mr. Wyndan, who was chairman of the board and ..."

Rick quickly opened one of the other two papers that were delivered each morning outside the door of his eighth-floor apartment. This one was the one he worked for, the *Montgomery County Daily Dispatch*. The story was front page, of course—it was a Montgomery County crime—under a three-column headline. And with a photo—Wyndan had the strong, cleanly-angled, handsome face of a stereotypical blue blood Main Liner. Fifty-eight, three married daughers, four grandchildren. His wife Eva had been visiting one of their daughters, who'd driven her to meet him at the club, where he was awarded the 50-to-60-year-old's inter-club championship trophy.

Call me Charlie. He'd said that when Rick called him Mr. Wyndan. And he said it with a few quick nods of his head, a smile and a firm handshake, as if emphasizing that he meant it. The few company brass Rick met that day did call him Charlie.

Rick had interviewed him about a plan that NCI set up to offer psychological help to employees and their families for his column four months ago. It was in his rather spartan executive suite, spartan that is, for a corporate headquarters that took up two square blocks several miles outside Philly, and included a separate division or two, such as industrial dyes.

Which was one of the reasons, though he'd heard the rumors, Rick was surprised when NCI laidoff over five hundred of its 2,500-some employees a couple of months later.

Rick never saw Wyndan again, though he did hear from him twice. The first was to say how much he appreciated the writeup. The second came a couple of weeks after the layoffs.

Rick had just published a column dealing with the emotional impact of the massive corporate "downsizing" going on in the country. Basically an interview with a psychiatrist, it focused primarily on violence that layoffs have been known to trigger—from crime in the workplace to suicide and family abuse. And the psychiatrist honed in on a highly-publicized phenomenon that he believed could exacerbate it—companies whose stock skyrocketed and whose CEO incomes still ballooned as they laidoff workers.

Although the column didn't name any company, NCI was a prime example of that phenomenon.

The column touched something in a lot of people—it brought in more than the usual mail and phone calls. None had been critical of the column, except Wyndan himself, and then only in a way. He'd called, ostensibly, to ask if Rick ever accepted speaking engagements. When Rick said he did, Wyndan said he would have someone get back to him. (But "someone" never did, so it could have been just an excuse to get across a point.) At the end of the conversation he'd said the column was "interesting."

But then, after a pause, "I just hope it doesn't give anyone ideas."

That morning as always, Terri took a shower, washed her hair, towel-dried it and herself, then went to the bureau to pick out a bra and bikini panties. Hers were mostly black, though differentiated by a variety of little brightly-colored patterns and designs. The panties she selected had a red rose toward the right side, the bra a thin red arc under each cup.

She sat in front of the mirror over the vanity and blow-dried her hair, pulling at it between her fingers all the while so it would stay wild and a little curled. Then she brushed blush on her cheeks, pencilled on eyeliner and put on lipstick and then lip gloss. She pulled on the same jeans as yesterday, leaving them partly unzipped while she searched her closet for the right blouse. She slipped it on, then her hands behind her neck, fastened the clip of her turquoise beaded necklace. Her hand then went through her costume jewelry box again, selected the drop earrings with the plastic red hearts.

Only the release of a long deep breath revealed anything of her tension. But it was much less than when she first woke up, was almost under control.

She bent down at the closet for shoes. Her eyes went immediately to her sneaks, but then after some hesitation she put on high heels. Nothing was going to happen; you've got to think nothing's going to happen. She took her handbag off the top of the vanity, holding it by the strap, then jiggled it to feel its weight before slipping it onto her shoulder.

She stopped at the head of the stairs. There was the smell of fresh coffee, and she could hear her parents' voices. She'd hoped her mother had gone to work—she worked two days a week as a receptionist for a podiatrist and was looking for a fulltime job; she'd just hoped that her father had gone *somewhere*.

They were at the kitchen table. They both looked over at her, her mother saying, "Morning," her father nodding, then looking away and putting a lit cigarette to his mouth. She said, "Morning."

She went to the hall closet and pulled out her down jacket from the press of coats. Her mother called, "You don't want any breakfast?"

"No, I'm a little late."

But she lingered by the closet. Her heart had begun beating hard. It hadn't last night—she'd fallen easily into a deep sleep—nor even this morning when she woke up tense. But it was really going now.

She'd just seen the morning paper folded next to him by his plate. It had to be in there, he had to have seen it, but what was he talking about, he was saying something about his brother's wife. And her mother was saying something about her too, and he was saying, "Well, what do you expect?"

Like nothing had changed in his world. Like there was nothing that should keep him grinning and calling his old buddies all day.

Unless it wasn't in there yet.

She zipped up the jacket, but then still lingered. She took

down a woolen scarf and curled it around her throat—it was supposed to be much colder today.

And then she heard him say, after a long pause, "I'm telling you, I got to say it again. I got to say it again. There really is a God."

The creep was looking at her from his office like she was an hour late when it was maybe four minutes. She hung up her coat but for a few moments couldn't quite release her fingers from her handbag. Wherever she would put it under the counter wasn't just right—it was too far there; here, she would have to stay in this one spot all day and she couldn't. She settled it in between two stacks of returns slips, almost in dead center of the counter, giving it a last squeeze to feel the bulk in there before straightening up.

She felt calm, yet never more alert. Faces, things—everything seemed so clear.

People were starting to line up in front of her now.

"Shower curtains, sixth aisle on the left ... Andirons, eighth aisle ... Yes, just put it right there, do you have your sales slip ..?"

This was the last place she wanted to be today. She'd been tempted to call Denny and say let's take off, even knew where she wanted to go. But that was like losing control of something. She wanted to be right here, to see, to know, even though she hadn't looked at the paper, didn't want to read about it.

Toward noon, becoming anxious to know how Denny was, she called Quick Man Lube from the counter.

"Denny?" a voice she recognized as his boss' said. "You tell me where he's at. He didn't show up."

There was a slight tremor of her hand as she lowered the receiver. The manager was coming back up the aisle now and she wasn't supposed to make personal calls, but screw him,

she was calling Denny's place now. No answer. She hung up
and tried again, but still no answer. Where the hell was he?
They'd both said they'd go to work, no changing anything.
He said it, she said it.

If only she had wheels. Her car, an '86 Chevy Cavalier,
had been totaled, some old witch who should be in a *home*
had slammed into her. Yet *her* insurance would go up when
she got another car.

Where the hell was he?

Just before lunch—she was only going to have an apple—
she noticed something that sent a little wave of heat from her
heart. She moved quickly over to her handbag, not sure what
she'd do. A young guy wearing a topcoat and holding a briefcase, over by the light fixtures, was looking over at her.

She gave him one quick look, then turned away, the spurt
of anxiety fading. She knew *that* look, it was no cop's look.
She didn't mind guys giving her a look, she always liked it,
even found it difficult not to smile, but it had to be a real guy.
She and the girls knew this type, used to make fun of them
among themselves. The phonies. The fairies. Or their other
favorite word for them—bookworms.

Denny came into the store at twenty to five, and the instant
she saw him she knew everything was okay. He had that cocki-
ness about him she loved. He stood just inside the doorway
smoking a cigarette, even with red and white signs all around
saying NO SMOKING. He had a slight smile on his face. She knew
someone would go over to tell him, and she'd bet he would smile
and take several long puffs before slowly walking out.

Which is what happened: a stock boy came over, but the
way the stock boy was talking to him it was as though with
admiration. And Denny nodded and took a puff or two, deep.
Then he looked at her with a smile and walked out.

That's what had attracted her to him. It had been three or four days after she broke up with Greg and she'd been sitting at the counter at Turner's when she saw him come in with a couple of other guys. She used to see him occasionally in school, but had never spoken to him, thought about him or even known he'd dropped out. But there was something about him then that made her glance at him twice: the way he stood, one shoulder slightly down; the way he smoked. He was thinner than most guys she liked, though he had broad shoulders, and not as tall—he was no more than five-ten to her five-eight. But real dude-looking, real cool. So cool she was afraid he wouldn't think she was, that he'd seen her glance at him; and so when Joanie leaned over to say something to her, she didn't want to because he'd think they were talking about him.

And then he was sitting next to her, turned to her, an elbow on the counter. And it came out of a perfectly straight face, "You happen to have a cigar?"

And she and Joanie, after a look at each other to see if he was crazy, just broke up like *kids*.

She went riding with him that afternoon. He'd been working for a tree service, he liked to go high up, but something happened that one of the other guys, a favorite of the boss, didn't like and the two of them had a fistfight. And Denny beat him up and was fired. He wasn't in any hurry about taking another job, he'd told her; he hated to take shit, he'd said, and wouldn't. And almost right away she felt about him what she felt about herself, though she'd never really formed it into words: that somehow everything would work out for him; more than work out, that something no one could even think of right now, something magic would happen.

And one of the things she'd liked was that he didn't try to come on strong that first day, just tried to kiss her in the car, and he kept laughing with her when she kept turning her face in every direction, and he would make gobbling and blowing sounds with his lips on her arched neck.

The following afternoon he was waiting for her outside school and they had some grass in his car, only about a block away, then went up to his room over the flower shop. He brought out a quart of Bud, which was not quite filled, and surrounded by all his rock and stock car driver posters, they took turns at it. But she took only a few swallows, and he took only a few more, then he went to his closet. He came back with the twenty-two handgun.

They'd been talking about kids getting mugged and murdered, and he brought this out and said he took it everywhere he went. He'd bought it, he was sure it was a stolen job, he'd said, from a nigger in North Philly he'd been sent to. The funny thing, he'd said, was that if he ever had to use it, and he wouldn't hesitate, let someone just *try* something, if he ever had to use it it would probably be on a nigger.

She didn't like that word. And a big part of the reason probably was that there'd been two black girls she'd been real friendly with at St. Francis who were so nice. And it wasn't as if she wouldn't mind blacks living on her street, she would. And if she had to give up everyone who said nigger, she would hardly have any friends. So it wasn't a big thing, if anything at all, against him.

The next thing he brought out was a paperback copy of some almanac, and he went through it to see if he could find statistics on which country had the most murders, but stopped to read her something about Australia, then about chess champions; he'd like to teach her chess someday if she was interested.

He never once lost any of that cool; she found it hard to believe he'd picked her out. So later, lying on the bed the sofa turned into, she was a little surprised during his first kiss that his heart was booming and even seemed to be skipping beats against her. She was so calm she was aware of every single beat, was even a little frightened for him. Yet somehow it was *nice*. And he didn't force himself either: when after kissing her and touching her all over like a wild man, he had some trouble doing it at first, said pleadingly, "Touch me, babe ... that's it, that's it," she didn't mind that at all, either.

He didn't seem to have any great trouble with it again. But there was something she sensed just under his surface that helped draw her closer to him, and made her feel sure he wouldn't leave her.

He smiled at her from his car, parked right at the curb. She got in, said angrily, "Where were you?"

"Where was I what?" He looked hurt.

"Don't give me that, I called you. Work. Home."

He pulled in a breath. "Look, I had trouble makin' myself go in. I know, I know, I should have. And I wish I had. My mother's husband called me—first at work, then there. 'When you comin' to see your mother? When you comin' to see your mother?' The son of a bitch! All of maybe twenty-nine!"

Terri watched him light a cigarette, glowering. He hadn't seen his mother since his father died seven months ago, in a rooming house in New York. A poor, good-natured slob, Denny called him.

"Anyway"—and the swagger was back in him—"I went and got something. A three fifty-seven Magnum." His thumb jerked toward the glove compartment. Then, with a half-smile, "You saw the papers."

"No."

"No? Look." He reached to the back seat and brought two

over. She saw part of the headline on one of them, part of the face. She opened it just enough to see the full face. She stared at it, feeling nothing for him, just a residue of hate.

"It's really great," Denny was saying, his voice a swift whisper, as though someone were in the car with them. "Really great. They think it was robbery."

It took several seconds for that to sink in. And then her reaction was like a silent shout: *Robbery? Robbery! The whole world should know why!*

Chapter Five

That morning Rick turned into the drive leading up to the *Dispatch*'s two-story, near-white stone building some twenty miles from the city. He gathered up his briefcase and coat, a short loden-green canvas job he bought in London and only wore in the sharpest cold, and carried it over his arm now even though it wasn't all that cold.

Harry, a security guard just inside the lobby, went into the hint of a wrestler's stance—an ex-wrestler, he knew Rick had wrestled in high school and college—and smiled. It was a daily routine, except when Rick came in with someone. Maxine, a middle-aged black woman at the reception desk, said, her face bright, "My aunt said to remember to thank you. She's going to call them."

"Good." Maxine had asked him, for her aunt, how to go about getting free psychiatric nurse help at home.

His office was on the second floor, in the features department across the hall from the newsroom. He hung up his coat and sports jacket—he had on a denim shirt, beige slacks and, for a change, socks with his Docksiders, white athletic socks—and made a half-hearted stab at his short rumpled hair before attacking his mail. There were a couple of dozen news releases, mostly from psychiatric facilities and organizations; some letters and e-mail from psychiatrists, psychologists and one psychiatric social worker, drawing attention to their own work or suggesting a topic for a column or, in one case, criticizing the approach of a psychologist he'd interviewed; and a thick handful of mail from readers, most of them thanking him for help they derived from a column.

Occasionally, as he went through them, he looked across the hall. From here he could see Joe Cooperman's desk, in the line fronting all the other desks in the partially-filled room. Cooperman wasn't there behind his computer as yet.

Cooperman was covering the Wyndan murder.

Rick drew over his wastepaper basket, dumped in whatever were easily dumpable releases, set aside letters to be answered—he answered every one that gave an address—and made a note on those that might lead to columns.

Whenever he thought of it, which was less now but still fairly often, it seemed like a hundred years ago that he'd been an investigative reporter. It was in Tampa, on the second paper he'd worked on since college. He was tapped for investigative work when he was just twenty-six, made a bad name for himself among assorted lowlifes in high and low places, thought he would stay there until the *New York Times* or *Washington Post* came after him, but then five years ago the rumors came true and the paper folded. He was thirty-three then, married, and it wasn't until he was thirty-four and divorced that he got another job—doing PR and putting out a newsletter for a psychiatric hospital in Miami. It was on-the-job training in the field, and it led to his meeting the features editor of the *Dispatch* at the annual convention of the American Psychiatric Association, which led to a few drinks, some exchange of thoughts about a possible column on pop psychology written in everyday language, some sample columns, and then an offer. That was a little more than two years ago.

He wrote three columns a week now, just about all of them interviews. Child abuse, teen problems, sex, divorce, self-esteem, feminism, male bonding, father-sons, father-daughters, mother-sons, mother-daughters, youngest sibling, oldest sibling, middle sibling, inter-racial marriage, old parents, parent abuse—the topics, though seemingly destined to run out, were endless in their variations. Although he swore he was never going to be a damn Miss Lonelyhearts, would never attempt to answer readers' problems himself, the columns were aimed directly at the reader. *You wake in the dead of night and wonder if you're the only one who ... Well, I had a chat the other day with Dr.—* And occasionally he would work in himself—his divorce, the pain of it at the time; writer's block; his having had to adapt to changes in his career; but always with one or more authorities to comment and expand on it.

And he turned out to be good at it—the column had taken off right away, was on its way to being syndicated nationally, and had recently led to a book contract.

He was on the phone now when he saw Cooperman come in, take off his coat, disappear with it, then come back and sit down at his desk. A few minutes later, waiting until Cooperman finished talking to the guy at the next desk, he went over to him.

Cooperman, a bearish man, acknowledged him with a slight lift of his brows.

"You have a couple minutes?"

"Yeah." Cooperman was one of those still giving him a bit of a frosty reception after all this time: a new guy being handed a column when there were people here for years. And on psychiatry!—Rick had overheard some of the remarks.

"About Wyndan," Rick said. "Do the cops seem sure it was attempted robbery?"

"They say." Cooperman's hands, folded on his lap, opened a little though the fingers remained intertwined.

"I was wondering. Did anything come up about the guy just getting out and shooting him before trying to rob him?"

Cooperman looked at him. He said, almost rhythmically, "I guess there are those who shoot first and there are those who rob first."

"Oh. Really." Rick looked at him, nodding. He'd asked for this; he should have known. And it wasn't just this. The guy was probably six-two, maybe two hundred fifty pounds, to his five-eleven, one sixty-seven; but he'd love to have this slob alone.

"Look," Cooperman said, "they've been doing this for years. They may not be big on kids really wanting to screw their mothers, but murder they know."

Rick just kept looking at him, then walked away.

Several minutes later, typing at his computer, he looked up to see that Cooperman had materialized in his doorway. He was standing with his folded arm across the jamb, his forehead on his wrist.

"You want, see a detective named Zinn. A pretty nice guy."

"Thanks."

Cooperman, his head still on his wrist, opened the hand. Then he walked back to his desk.

It was suddenly, Rick thought, like they bowled together every week.

Rick tried to concentrate on his next column, this one on narcolepsy, the embarrassment and guilt so many of these people feel; but after a few minutes he still couldn't get his mind completely on it.

I just hope it doesn't give anyone ideas ...

That was crap. And the worst part was that Wyndan hadn't let him answer: he'd simply said it and then—you could almost see a little smile—said goodbye and hung up.

Like he wanted Rick to twist over it.

But he didn't twist then and he wasn't twisting now. He felt sorry for Wyndan and his family, and anger at the crime—but responsibility, none. His column had just expressed a psychiatrist's thoughts and fears—hardly even new ones—of what could happen, of what was already happening. But it wasn't just a scare piece. What Dr. Crane did was offer advice on often subtle signs of serious depression and potential violence that relatives, friends and the unemployed person should be alert to; that it was important to communicate among each other and go for professional help, starting perhaps with one's family doctor or clergyman.

But there was one letter Rick received that he was thinking about, and certain calls ...

He didn't save most of the letters he got from readers—his office would be overflowing—but he did save copies of his replies in his computer.

Most of the letters he got on this one, as he recalled, were to thank him for the column, or to invite him to give a talk, or to share a bitter experience and their way of resolving it, or the help that had come from God. But this letter, bearing a Philly P.O. box number, was quite different.

Rick pulled his reply to it up on the screen:

Dear Mr. Takoni:

Thank you for your letter. I am glad you think enough of me to write. Now my hope is that you will trust me. Will you call me? If I'm not in, leave a message when you will call back and I will make every effort to be here.

I am also glad you think enough of me to admit that you haven't used your right name. You don't ever *have* to give me your right name. Just call so we can talk. It can be strictly on the phone or if you'd like we can meet. I assure you that nothing you say will go past me.

I look forward to hearing from you.

Sincerely,

Rick Broder

The only reason Rick could think of that "Takoni" had given a return address, even though just a box number, was that his letter was a cry for help. But he never did hear from him, even though Rick had done something he never did before—ran an italicized appeal at the bottom of his column for Takoni to contact him again. And then he'd done something else he'd never done—the letter seemed so psychotic, the guy was going to "kill every boss he ever had"—that Rick turned it over to a cop he knew in Philly, which'd seemed to excite the guy as much as another gray day in February.

And then there were the two phone calls.

One was from a woman who gave the name Louise, said she was calling about her godson, who'd starting "acting funny" after he was fired recently, and was talking about "things" he was going to do to his former manager. She couldn't get him to see a psychiatrist and was hoping Rick might have better luck. So she was wondering if Rick would talk to him if she could get him to call. And though Rick agreed, that was the last he'd heard of it.

The other call he remembered even more clearly, partly because he'd been aware that her voice was muffled, that she must have been holding something over the mouthpiece. Her name, she'd said hesitantly, was Mary, and she read his col-

umn "every day." Someone in her family—she never said who—
was "going crazy." He had lost his job and kept saying he was
going to kill "them," meaning his "boss, his bosses." The reason she was calling was to find out if Rick could help her get
to see or even just talk to the doctor he'd interviewed, because
she didn't know if he saw "everyone."

Rick explained that Dr. Crane practiced in Baltimore and
that he'd be glad to give her his number, but if she'd like he
could recommend someone closer. He asked her where she
lived and, after some hesitation, she said Philadelphia. And
he recommended a psychologist, Jay Goldstein.

He hadn't heard from Goldstein, who probably would have
called or dropped him a note to thank him for the recommen-
dation if the woman had contacted him. But maybe not.

He checked his Rolodex now and called him. But he got
Goldstein's answering machine. He spoke to it.

"Jay. Rick Broder. Please call me when you can."

He sat, now, with his hand still on the phone. There was
one person who somehow had more information about more
people than anyone else he knew. He made the call. The familiar low, gruff voice answered.

Rick said, "Sam. This is Rick."

After a moment: "Oh." Then a long pause that might last
the day. And it was, Rick was sure, all a ploy. It gave him an
edge: *you* talk, you tell me things.

Rick said, "How are you? How's Aunt Esther?"

"Oh." This time he said it tiredly.

"Sam, I'd like to ask you something. Did you know Charles
Wyndan? At North Chemicals? The one—did you read it?—
who was murdered last night?"

Again a pause. Then, irritably, "I can't hear on this thing."

Which Rick had rather expected. It meant: Come over. It meant: You don't ever come over.

It wasn't true; he went there at least once a month or so. Sam was his father's older brother, seventy-eight or maybe - nine; his father would have been seventy-two now, his mother a year younger. His father, a pharmacist as was his mother—they had met in pharmacy school—had never seemed to quite get used to his brother being a private eye. He would brag about his exploits to friends and joke about his misadventures—like the time one of Sam's guys was doing some tailing and fell in a cesspool while walking in one direction, then fell into it again coming back—but both the bragging and joking were almost always with a roll of his eyes.

Although Sam used to do missing persons, security work, other things probably, he preferred, as his business card read, "marital work."

Used to. Now he only had an ex-cop in his sixties named Wally help him do whatever little work came their way.

His uncle and aunt's home was in West Philly, near the University of Pennsylvania. A three-story row brownstone, with apartments on the second and third floor rented out to students. A bronze plaque near the door said BRODER'S INVESTIGATIVE SERVICES, INC. To the left in the foyer was the thick oak door to their apartment; the door straight ahead, near the bank of mailboxes on the wall, led upstairs.

Sam opened the door. He used to be a little taller than Rick, but was slightly stooped now, and bald except for some strands of dark brown hair and side-fringe, which Rick was sure was dyed. Rick's father had been somewhat taller, leaner, far better looking, though in the last few years of his father's life Rick noticed the family resemblance.

Sam had an unlit cigar between the tips of his fingers by

his side, always had it, and now and then would put it to the front of his lips and draw in lightly. He lifted it to his mouth now as he looked at Rick. It was a dark room, even with lights on, and served as an office and living room, the desk at one end as massive as the furniture.

"You didn't bring her?"

"She couldn't come," Rick said, "she said to tell you she's sorry." Last month Sam had met the lady he was currently seeing; Rick had met her only the month before.

"I'd known that," Sam said, turning and walking to a chair, "I woulda heard you on the phone."

Rick smiled. Sam rarely did—just a trace at his own rare jokes, never at anyone else's. He sat down carefully on an upholstered straightback chair—he'd had a hip replacement nine months ago, had only recently stopped using a cane. Even as a kid, especially as a kid, Rick loved visiting him; liked to hear his stories, particularly about when he was a prizefighter; liked to look at his badge and hold it.

Rick could hear the clatter of plates in the dining room. He didn't want to eat here, he never did—his aunt was a terrible cook, the exact opposite of his mother, who had come here from Italy when she was a little girl and had been a gourmet cook at "Jewish," as well as just about everything else. But Sam had said sternly, "Come, you'll come."

Rick walked into the dining room. Sam's third wife, she looked even older than him, was short, bow-legged under her long dark dress, and rarely talked. As usual, she gave a quick little smile, but said nothing and continued setting the table. She and Sam didn't have any children. His only children were from his first wife, one living in California, the other in Cleveland.

The soup, it turned out, wasn't bad, but the sliced brisket

was almost black, the mashed potatoes too thin and creamy. Sam kept his cigar on the table by him. He'd had one quick shot of whisky, a swallow followed by a torn-off piece of rye bread, before starting to eat, which reddened his cheeks, and he ate heartily. Rick sipped at some not-quite-sweet red wine.

"So Ricky," his uncle said, over tea. He'd been talking about Rick's parents' drugstore, how everyone thought at first they were crazy when they got rid of the fountain and made it strictly a pharmacy.

Rick said, "I was wondering do you know anything about this fellow Wyndan."

Sam didn't ask why; it wasn't his way. He thought, then said, "I know this—I'd buy stock any company he ran. A brain. I wouldn't have played poker with him, I'll tell you that, boychik. But I'll tell you something else he was. He was a big, big *tuckus* man." Aunt Esther, who was stacking a few dishes to take into the kitchen, didn't even glance at him. "But most of these big money guys are *tuckus* men. You think athletes have women running after 'em? These big money guys, I mean the *big* ones ..." Sam put the cigar to his lips.

Rick said, "Let me tell you why I'm asking about him." He told Sam about the calls from Louise and Mary, which were like part of the air now, and about turning Takoni's letter over to a cop in Philly.

"He didn't exactly jump up and down, and I never heard anything. But I'm curious. Is there any way to find out the guy's real address?"

Sam looked at him. "I don't know if you know, but if a box's for a business, you're allowed to know the address. But that's no business. Anyway, you got a couple weeks? The reason I say, I got a source who's got access"—he liked using formal words—"but what can I tell you, he's away. He comes back, if you still want we'll get it."

"Well, we'll see."

"Let me tell you something," Sam said after a little pause. "With all the crazies around, if I was head of a big business I'd be praying Wyndan was killed by a husband, a mugger. Anyone but someone who was laidoff."

*C*HAPTER SIX

Terri couldn't make herself get out of bed. And even whenever she did she wasn't going to work.

She was supposed to go in today, Saturday; she'd had off Monday. But it was gray out, miserable, and she'd just be evening things up; they owed her plenty of time, all those times she'd leave ten, fifteen minutes late. She lay on her back, with her arm across her eyes. There was a slight racing in her and she couldn't get her mind away from it, couldn't fall back to sleep. But she still wasn't going in.

She got up soon and looked out the window. It was no less gray, but now there was something nice about it. She knew where she wanted to go.

Putting on her robe she went downstairs. Her parents were in the living room, so she went to the phone in the kitchen.

Her voice low, she said, "You working today?"

"I don't even know I got a job," Denny said.

"Call them, tell 'em you're still sick. I want to get out of here. Let's go someplace."

There was a pause, then he said, "I'll see you."

"Soon. Get here soon."

When Denny pulled up to the curb the first thing he said, his face anguished, was, "Something wrong?"

"Nothing's wrong. I just want to get outta here."

"Man, you scared the shit out of me," he said, shaking his head.

He didn't say anything when she asked could she drive; just moved over. She drove a couple of blocks before he said, "Where we goin'?"

"The Poconos? I thought the Poconos. I just want to get out of here."

"Sure." He said it eagerly.

It wasn't until they were on the Schuylkill Expressway, were able to go fast, that she felt something lift from her. She turned on the radio, began scrambling for some good rock, then let him take over. He tuned into the middle of an old one, "Bitch Betta Have My Money," had it blasting now, was slapping at his thighs when he thought of cigarettes. He lit his, put one in her mouth and held his lighter to her as she bent over. "Straight Jackin" was on now, and he was drumming the top of the dash, while for the first time in so long, rock was doing it to her. She grinned at him, and he grinned back and slapped the dash hard.

The gray, snappy-cold day was just perfect, it could mean snow. She hoped it would snow like hell.

They were on the Turnpike soon, and from there the Extension, taking them north. They cut off on 22 to go east, then north again, on 33. They stopped once and had hamburgers and fries and sodas; she pulled out of the gravel parking lot fast.

Several cars had skiis on top of them. No new snow here yet, just some patches of old snow along the side of the road.

She passed another car with skiis on it and a kid behind the wheel who gave them the finger, and several minutes later Denny said, "Oh shit."

She saw it too, late. A cop car. Parked diagonally in a little opening in the woods.

"Oh shit," Denny said again. "But maybe—" Then he looked over his shoulder, and she at the rearview mirror, and saw the car pulling out. She started to slow up, but he said, "Oh Christ, the—" which meant the guns—she'd forgotten!—he pulled open the glove compartment. "Ditch 'em," he yelled at her, "throw yours out, I'll throw this one!" and her foot went hard on the gas, until she realized there was no way to get rid of them, the cop would see.

"Put it back!" she yelled.

He stared at her, then put it back. She pulled over onto the shoulder.

"He opens it," Denny was saying, his voice quivering, "he sees yours, I swear to God—"

"Shut up!" Her glare seized him. But she herself didn't know what she'd do. But just for a few seconds. Go for it, she'd go for it!

The patrol car drew up behind them. It was several moments before she saw the door open and the legs and then the full body of the cop come out. A state trooper.

She grabbed her bag from the back seat and put it next to her. Now she turned off the radio and lowered the window. He leaned in, a big man with a wide face under the wide, hard brim. He looked at them, then around the interior of the car, then back at her.

"You trying to get away there? Good thing you changed your mind."

"No, sir. I mean, I got scared, my foot hit the pedal ... I'm going to get such hell," she said, holding her mouth and shaking her head.

"You were going seventy-three in a thirty-five mile an hour zone." He kept staring back and forth at them. Then, to her, "Where you going?"

"Lake Wallenpaupack."

"What're you doing there?"

"Just ... going there. Taking a ride."

"Seventy-three is a lot more than a ride." He kept looking at her, then asked for her license.

He went back to his car with it. Denny stared at her. His lips silently mouthed the words, "You're doing good," as if their car might be bugged. Then, after at least five minutes, his lips said, "What do you think?" His fingers were rubbing at each other. She shook her head. All she knew was she wasn't going to panic. Whatever happened, she wasn't going to panic. She kept looking back. Now he was rising up out of the car again and coming toward them. She lowered the window again and he bent over and handed her a ticket and her license.

"You want to drive fast, that fast, you stay home. Don't come up here for that. You could kill a kid." He glared at her, then waved her on and went back to his car.

He was waiting, she saw, until she pulled out.

It was about five miles before she stopped seeing him follow them.

She looked at Denny, her heart still knocking, and pulled in a long, slow breath. She'd been sure that at any second something about her driving, or some new suspicion right out of the air, would bring the cop speeding up to them again. Denny's eyes were searching her face. He'd been sitting stiffly, afraid to do more than dart a few glances at the rearview mirror, as though the cop could see into the car and would take everything as suspicious. But as she began to smile, so did he. Then she leaned forward against the wheel and began to laugh, all her tension coming out with it. Denny began laughing too, then threw his head back and kept shaking it as he let out a howl.

Once in a while little specks of snow dotted the windshield, but none had for the past half hour. Terri kept wishing for it, but it didn't matter any more, it just felt good being up here. The road, climbing and dipping and leveling off, curved through crossroad hamlets, miles of winter-stark trees, an occasional billboard giving directions to a resort or some natural wonder.

She slowed up and took one of the small roads cutting through the woods toward the lake. There was a scattering of houses on either side, back among the trees, far apart from each other, some quite grand, some cabins or A-frames. They looked dark, even in the daylight, and deserted—she saw only one with a car parked by it.

She turned off on another lane. It was bumpy here, isolated. She slowed up even more, then stopped at the only house there, a large, one-story house of stone and wood and glass, with a wide deck on pilings facing the lake. She knew every room in it.

The lake was calm, clear. You could just about see the other side from here. She got out to stretch her legs, and Denny followed. She went close to the lake. Other solitary houses jutted out toward it from the woods.

She looked up at their house: the Devores', though she'd heard they'd put it up for sale several years ago.

She was ten when Robin, who was new in the class, had invited her here for two weeks. Mr. Devore, who was head of some kind of business, had driven her up; his family was already there. She remembered him smiling at her across his shoulder as he drove, even some of his jokes; wanting to know about her favorite subjects, TV shows. Then the fishing, swimming, the Devores' small sailboat; barbecues out on the deck; the whole, friendly family; she and Robin sharing a room.

She was up here a couple of more times after that, but then the Devores must have blamed her, since she'd been going steady with Tommy's best friend and introduced her;

blamed her for Robin, who always had her hand up in class, being found in the park doing it with Tommy.

No one ever came right out and said it, but nobody had to; Robin avoided her the rest of the year, and next fall went to a high-class Catholic academy.

She hated the thought of Robin, it made her want to puke; but this place, not the exact house so much, but the place ... In fact, the summer after it was over with Robin she'd had her mother and father drive up and look to see if they could rent somewhere, but her father said, "What do you do in the woods, what do you do here?" So they'd gone to Jersey again, Ocean City, which she liked, but she'd wanted at least one more time here. She often daydreamed of it, especially when she had problems. And though she never drove up here alone, she drove up a few times with friends, though she never got sloppy with them about it; it was just, you know, a ride.

She didn't with Denny now, either.

He said, nodding quickly, "Nice." But he was hunched together, shivering a little.

They got back in the car. She let him take over the driving, directing him down several other lanes to the lake, then down an asphalt road to a deserted summer camp, the entrance chained. From here you could see some of the cabins, the flagpole on a knoll; she remembered visiting a kid here with the Devores, counselors waving and whistling, and kids running down to the lake.

Denny said, "Gettin' hungry."

They drove to a little village several miles away, then through it to a diner, where they were the only ones except for a guy on a stool, who looked at them and went behind the counter. They both had grilled cheese and bacon and fries, then went back into town and went into an arcade, where there were several kids, and they played a few games.

Outside, she said, "Let's stay over."

"I don't know how much money ..." He looked in his wallet. He had twenty-six dollars; she had thirty-eight.

She knew of a motel a few miles down the road. It was on a hill overlooking the lake, but she was afraid it would be too expensive. She waited in the car while he went in. She could tell by the way he was walking back that it was a no.

"Seventy-five bucks!" he said, climbing in. "Christ, they only got two cars!" He gestured toward cars on the parking lot.

She wondered what to do. She didn't want to go back. She wished the hell it would snow, a blizzard that would block the way. She thought of all those deserted houses. It would be so easy ...

She told him to keep driving, in a direction that was taking them farther from home. They passed a shutdown rifle range, a cruddy auto repair shop that also sold gas—they would have to fill up again before driving back—then through another village. A few miles outside was a sign that said CABINS. There was a small house that was the office, and several cabins behind it, on a slight hill.

This time Denny came back, smiling. "Thirty-five bucks."

It was cold in the pinewood cabin; the heat was almost off. Denny raised the thermostat on the wall and almost immediately the heat started coming in. Terri sat on the bed, still in her jacket, then hung it on a rack. All she needed now to feel perfect was a good shower.

She stayed in it a long time, the water running hard; bent her hair to it, then flinging her head back, kept turning as it beat on her body. She came out naked, with a towel around her hair. She climbed into bed, was half under the covers before she was aware that Denny was standing over her, his face a grimace.

"It's goin' wrong." He gestured toward the TV. The news was on. "They're lookin' into other things. The layoffs—"

"Turn it off!" She sat up, the cover against her breasts. When he came back she said, "You and your television! Newspapers! Why the hell you readin', watchin'!"

She flung herself back, glowering. He stood there, then sat on the edge of the bed. "Reading, watching TV." Her heart was going fast. Asshole! She let herself concentrate only on the rising and falling of her chest. She could feel herself calming. Soon her hand tugged at him and he lay back. She held onto his hand, looking at the ceiling.

She wondered what would happen if she told him what she was suddenly thinking. Wondered would he say no, be too scared to reason with. She started to say "Den," but instead raised herself up on one elbow and looked down at his face. Smiling, she stroked his forehead, his hair. His eyes took in her face, every part of it, with a kind of awe, then he lifted himself and lowered her to him.

Later as he lay next to her smoking, she said, "Den. I've been thinking. We've got to do someone else."

It was perfectly logical to her. And once something was logical to her there was no other way. She tried to explain it to Denny while Denny smoked, his forehead furrowed, his whole face worried.

"See, the only way you can get it away from there, the layoffs, is do someone else. That'll make it like it was anyone in the whole world who could have done it. See? Don't you see?"

She looked at him for a reaction, then suddenly was brushing burning cigarette ash off the sheet. "Christ, you're going to burn us up."

He was brushing at it quickly himself. Then he squeezed out his cigarette in an ashtray but only to take another one from the crumpled pack next to it on the night table. Terri took one, also. She drew in, looking at him. She was jumpy herself, but he mustn't know.

He let out a stream of smoke, squinting, thinking. Then, quietly, "Who?"

She woke in the dead of night. She hadn't had any dreams, at least any she remembered, and she didn't feel nervous, but she simply woke up. His bare back was to her, and she put her arm over him and came close. But she still felt a mile away from sleep. She'd told him, "We can do anyone." She hadn't spelled it out, but it could be anyone walking along at night, anyone parked at a red light, anyone coming out of a 7-Eleven, anyone waiting for a bus at a corner. Anyone at all.

She thought he was waking up, but it was only to shift position slightly. Her arm still lay over him. After a while she got up and went to the window. It was totally black out. Even the motel sign had been turned off. She lit a cigarette and exhaled against the window. She was aware now that though she hadn't thought she was nervous, she really was. But several minutes later she felt it easing away.

The thought had come in an instant, all by itself, but it was completely relaxing her. She didn't know who. But it had to be someone she hated, not just anyone.

She was sure of it on the ride home the next day. It couldn't, for instance, be a Mrs. Gionelli unloading packages from her car, it couldn't be the guy in the car they just passed, it couldn't be this lady at the tollbooth, it couldn't even be—though maybe—the trucker who pulled up right behind them with a blast of his horn, and Denny put far behind.

The cold gray of the day had darkened into evening as they pulled up in front of her house. Denny lowered the radio.

He said, "You sure?"

"Not tonight. Okay?" She bent over and kissed him on the cheek, then the mouth. His arms came around her.

He wanted her to stay over his place, and while a part of her wanted to, most of her didn't. It was important to her she go in that house here, maybe to see if anything had gone ... wrong, maybe just to get it over with, the hell she was sure she was going to get from her parents.

But most of all she felt a great need to be by herself.

"I'll call you later," she said.

He drew her to him again and they kissed.

She said, "You okay?"

It was the closest either of them came to saying anything more about doing someone else since they'd gotten in the car to come home.

All she'd said that morning was, "I was thinking, we'll think of something, we'll decide. We'll see." And that had lighted his face. Like it was something far off that might never happen.

Now he said, "Sure I'm okay. Why?"

"I'll call you later," she said.

She was on the staircase going up to her room when her mother took form behind her, from the living room.

"Tell me," she said, "what did I do?"

Terri looked at her. "What? Nothing."

"What did I do? Tell me. For God's sake, please tell me."

"Ask her," her father said from the living room, "what did I do to her?"

"What did I do to you?" her mother asked again.

Her father came out and glared at her mother. "Why's it always you? What did I do to her? She'll *talk* to you, she'll say a *word*!"

"Jack, please."

"Jack please, shit! I'm fucking sick of it!"

Terri started up the stairs, but his words stopped her.

"Listen to me! You listen to me!" His chest was heaving. "I never use that language! Never! But you drive me crazy! But you just listen! I don't care if you never talk to me. I don't *want* you to talk to me anymore. Lady, don't you blame me for you having to live here. I didn't ask you! But I'll tell you this. You stay here, you want to stay out all night, you call! You hear me? You'll call! If not, then get out! You hear me? Leave me alone, leave us alone, just get out!"

"Jack!" her mother cried, whirling on him. "Stop that! Stop it!"

Terri ran up the stairs, banged the door closed.

One of the last things she heard was her mother screaming, "*I'm* crazy? *You're* crazy! You know it?—you're crazy!"

She sat on the bed, half-expecting him to fling open the door—the lock was broken.

She just wished she had a knife.

She could almost feel the silence, now, down there. The yelling abruptly over, her parents had stopped speaking to each other. She could tell they were even in different rooms: almost the same time that she heard a familiar creaking in the living room, she heard the refrigerator door open and close, undoubtedly her father getting a beer.

Her breathing was still hard and she lay on the bed, still fully clothed, staring at the ceiling. Why she was breathing so hard had nothing to do with them anymore. It was the cops, they had come back in her mind as though rising from behind a bush. They would figure it out, they always did, they'd come here after her ...

But she just couldn't think things out.

It might have to be an "anyone" after all.

But then, when she stopped trying to think, it came to her. And all the good feelings of anger with it. Someone she just remembered her mother saying something about a few days ago. Someone she'd just about blanked out on.

A year ago her friend Molly asked if she'd like a part-time job. Molly worked off and on for a caterer, and there was an affair that evening and one of the girls had just quit. She was sure Terri would fit into this girl's uniform, which was just a black dress, white shirt, black bowtie and black shoes. And about six-thirty that evening Terri had gone to this estate which went on forever, made Wyndan's look like shit.

She wasn't made waitress, like Molly was, but stayed in the kitchen, chopping stuff and washing and taking out trash. This old piece of shit started coming into the kitchen, an old guy about seventy—he could have been a million—and he would put his face into the girls', grinning; and then when he saw her his eyes got this big. And later when she was outside with the trash, there he was in his tuxedo, white-haired and slightly bent, looking at her with a smile and smoking a cigarette. Then he came over and put his hand on her arm, that *old* hand—it was *disgusting*, it almost made her sick—and said, "Dear, do you do this full-time?"

"No."

"Where about do you live?"

She gestured vaguely, couldn't think what to say. "Over near the city."

"Well, if you ever want to look into a new job, you call me. I'm quite serious."

She was afraid to squirm away, it was *his* house and he might make up some lie, but she knew if he didn't get away from her she'd claw his eyes out and kick his balls right through his mouth.

"You hear?" he said. But just then someone called from the house, "Ed?" and he winked at her and walked away.

She wished she had her gun deep in his frightened little mouth right now!

*C*HAPTER SEVEN

Rick was a little surprised to see how much damage still remained from the storm of a few months ago. It had narrowed the beach by more than half and steepened the dunes and flattened most of the wired palings around them. Broken clamshells, ripped clean by the gulls, scattered the narrow streets leading up to the beach; they lay very white on the asphalt and even on the decks of some of the houses. There were only six houses on this street, three on each side. All had the vacant look of summer houses in winter.

The ocean was a dark gray-green, mostly gray. It curled to the beach almost silently, fanning out on the sand.

"I thought there'd be big waves today with this wind," Deirdre said.

"No, the size of waves is inverse to the wind," Rick said.

"Really?" She looked at him.

"No. I just like the way that sounds."

"Fun-ny." She put her arm through his.

They were standing on top of a dune, his car parked in front of the sign that said among other things:

NO DOGS, NO PICNICKING, NO BEVERAGES

He said, "You cold?"

"Let me just fix this." She pulled the drawstrings of her hood tighter. "Ah. Fine." Her corduroy jeans were tucked into boots. "Okay."

He took her hand, bracing her, and they started down the dune, sliding a little. "I hope we don't need beach badges," he said.

"You must be freezing." She squeezed his hand, as though she could test it through her glove.

He could barely remember the last time he wore a hat, couldn't remember at all ever wearing gloves. "Freezing? I'm burning up—need a popsicle."

They were down now, walking to the ocean, then holding hands turned and walked slowly toward the jetty on their far right. A lone seagull, its feathers fluttering in the wind, stood near some rotted timber tossed up by the ocean. It was staring rigidly at the water.

"Poor thing," she said, "I wonder what it's thinking."

"Who am I? What's it all mean?"

She laughed, turning to look back as they passed it.

This was something they'd promised themselves on the way here to Long Beach Island that they would do, no matter how windy, how cold.

"Sure," Bernie had said, "feel free, no formalities here, bring her."

Bernie was Bernie Frank, a child psychiatrist Rick had interviewed earlier that day about how parents might be able to detect or prevent school phobia. Bernie, whom Rick had interviewed several times before, was "easy," in that you turned on the tape recorder and pretty much let him soliloquize, except for an occasional question to move him in a direction you wanted. And so, while Deirdre was somewhere with Mrs. Frank, Bernie sat back in the study of their summer and occasional winter weekend home, overlooking a lagoon in the Loveladies section, and began expounding to him with gestures.

"You know," he said—he was a bawdy, husky guy who looked more like an ex-prizefighter than a child psychiatrist—"a lot of people have this idea of these kids screaming and ranting they don't want to go to school. You do have those kids, of course, but those parents know, or should know, there's a problem. But a lot of times these youngsters don't show obvious signs. And there *are* signs, but you have to know what to look for.

"For instance," he explained, "a kid stays home for a headache or an upset stomach or whatever. He may actually be staying home a lot with these sort of complaints, but the parents aren't aware he's really staying out more than the average youngster. They may think it's normal. Or they may not be aware that these complaints should be alerting them to a deeper problem. Or the parents may actually be encouraging these kids to stay out, by asking them every morning how they're feeling and having them stay home with almost every slight complaint.

"Something a lot of parents don't realize," he went on, "is that the problem can start in these kids at any age—they don't have to be just starting school. And what causes it?" Bernie loved rhetorical questions. "A lot of things. To get a little psychiatric, one is separation anxiety—there may be a lot of fighting going on at home, there may be other stresses in the family, and the kid has this need to be there. Or it could be something very realistic in school—maybe there's a bully he's afraid of."

Later, as the interview petered out, they'd talked for just a little while about other things—Bernie about his wines, Rick about a good beer he used to brew. And then as Rick stood up to go, it struck him that this guy was a close friend of Dr.

Goldstein, the psychologist he'd sent "Mary" to and whom he still hadn't heard from.

He said, "Would you happen to know if Jay Goldstein is out of town?"

"Yes. L.A. But he should be back in a day or two."

Rick and Dierdre walked as far as the jetty. There was a faint spray from the ocean, but it felt good. The houses facing the ocean behind the dunes looked cavernous in their emptiness. Until almost the day he died his father used to talk of the great buys they'd missed on the island. The climb back up the dune was a bit of a struggle; Deirdre toppled to her hands, but looked up laughing as he helped raise her up. In the car they both let go a big shiver, then he took her in his arms. She kept shivering against him.

"That was good," she whispered, "that was good, that was fun."

She let go another big shiver, but it was like the finale to fireworks, and he lifted her face and they kissed. She flattened her cheek against his and held onto him. He wished they could stay over, but she'd already told him she couldn't; she had a thirteen-year-old daughter, and the housekeeper would be leaving at eleven.

On the way home they decided to eat at his apartment. And he was selecting the menu, he said. They stopped at a supermarket, where he bought a pound of shrimp, cleaned and shelled, and a box of white rice while she picked out the things for a salad. He enjoyed food shopping at good stores; enjoyed feeling tomatoes, lifting things up, sniffing, reading labels. And it wasn't anything that had just come with being a bachelor; he'd done it when he was married, much to Carole's relief.

On the way to the checkout counter they remembered dessert, and they went to look at the fruit and she picked out an Israeli melon, winking as she held it to let him know she knew her stuff, too.

"This," he said at his sink, "is going to be, as you may have guessed, shrimp scampo."

"I think you mean shrimp scampi?" She was holding a glass of chardonnay, peering over it curiously; his Glenlivet on rocks was on the counter next to him.

"No. Scampo. At some point you're going to say 'oh.'"

"Oh?"

He looked at her with a smile. She was a little thing, just about came to his shoulders, with auburn hair—redder than his—freckles and wide, round glasses. She watched as he put the shrimp on a broiler tray and lightly floured them. Then he melted butter in a pan, added olive oil and scattered chopped garlic and parsley over them, with a touch of Worcester sauce. He drizzled it over the shrimp and put it in the broiler.

"You're not," she asked, "sautéing them?"

"No." He'd learned to play around with cooking early on, since his mother often had to work late. And she had taught him how, and the importance of simply not being afraid to experiment.

Deirdre looked at him, then said a deliberate, "Oh."

She had set the table, and about five minutes later he was jostling the shrimp out of the pan onto beds of rice.

He got her to her house ten minutes to eleven.

"Do I look disheveled?" she said in the car.

"I hope so."

They were both aware that they probably wouldn't be seeing each other for another week; she worked as a paralegal during the day and was going to law school three evenings a week. Though she felt guilty as hell about it costing her time with her daughter, she wasn't going to be caught the way she was when her husband walked out.

***

He went in to work on Sunday, just to pick something up. He looked through his mail, listened to his Voice Mail.

All the usual.

But then: "Mr. Broder," a man's voice said. "I hope to hell you feel mighty good about yourself. I knew Charlie Wyndan. I loved him. He was a dear friend, a good person, a great person. And I think what you wrote ... that column ... about crime— Right after they had to let those people go ..." The voice broke. "He told me himself what you wrote, it could make a terrible situation worse. But that poor guy, he didn't know how worse. I tell you you contributed to his death. You ... the whole goddamn media ..."

And it ended there.

CHAPTER EIGHT

There were so many things to do, it was as though she was running inside her skin. She'd had to force herself to come to work, she needed this money, but Christ, look what she had to see first thing, she was even a little *early*, is the creep staring bullets at her. Then, a worse warning sign, he was slowly lifting himself from his desk by his palms.

Deliberately turning away from him, Terri took off her high heels and put them under the counter.

His voice said, "So you're here." She looked at him. He was studying her face. "So you're really and truly here," he said. She didn't say anything. Just kept looking at him. "So you think you can just come in and go about like nothing happened." His head made a series of quick nods, his eyes always on her. "That right?"

"I didn't say that."

"You think you can just stay out, no call, then come in and everything's okay."

She'd forgotten to call. She'd remembered twice on the road to call in, but she'd forgotten it again after the first time she thought about it, and the second time it was after eleven and it was like too late, and she would think of something.

"You know," he said, "how many people who're looking for a job like this?"

Now this was scaring her. She had so many things to be scared about, and this was just shit, but she couldn't lose this job now. "I thought my mother called—"

"Aah," he said, swiping at the air. "I just can't have this. I had to pull Peggy off a register and she asked me why you were out and I had to say I didn't know. So how does that look? And you know this isn't the first time. And you know you promised me. And while I'm at it I want to bring this up, too. All the times you use the phone."

"I'm sorry." She hadn't wanted to say it—not to him, the creep, not to anyone, but especially now not to him. And it came out a little defiantly, which she needed.

"You're sorry." Sarcastic, but she sensed a little that she had him, that she was giving the filthy little creep who couldn't keep his eyes off her tits, her ass, a way of finally feeling big man over her. It was nearly sickening her, but she had to do it.

He was looking at her. She avoided his eyes, as if she didn't care, and quickly put on one shoe and started to put on the other as though ready to leave.

"Would you tend to this lady?" he said.

He looked at her as she slowly straightened up and faced a woman across the counter. He waited long enough to hear the woman's question, then he turned and walked back to his office.

At noon he was next to her again.

"And I don't want that anymore," he said with a slight jerk of his head. Denny stood by the doors, in front of the cash registers. "He can come in and shop or browse. But he can't just stand there."

***

Outside, Terri said, "What's the matter?" She knew that look.

"Lost my job," he said, almost over his shoulder, away from her. He walked over to his car and she followed and got in with him. He hit the steering wheel hard with the heels of his hands.

"'Three days,'" he said, imitating a voice, "'you're out three days.' *Shiit*."

"Did you ever call them?"

"I called. The first day. I said I was sick. You don't have to call every damn day, do you?" Ordinarily she might have given him hell. She looked at him as he turned away again, staring out his window. Then he hit the steering wheel again. "I come in early, plenty of times I come in early! And I stay late—plenty of times! Christ, these fuckin' people!" Again the steering wheel, this time with one fist. "You give 'em everything, you give 'em your life!"

She wanted to ask, "Did you say you were sorry?" But she was pretty sure he didn't; she couldn't remember ever hearing Denny tell another guy he was sorry. Anyway, it suddenly didn't matter. It had become even better this way. Den with this fury.

"Den," she said, and then when he finally looked over at her, "Den, you ever hear of a guy named Ed Henning?"

She hadn't been able to make the call during her lunch hour, the public phone on the wall in the drugstore stayed taken. And she wouldn't be able to make one from here, at the counter, though she felt a tugging toward that phone. But even if she could, she couldn't really talk from here, she wasn't even sure what to say.

But just to call, to see. It was something she had to do. And not tomorrow, not even this afternoon; *now*. But either the creep was here, or someone from the floor, or customers. Everyone wasn't away at the same time, until it was almost time for her to go.

She didn't realize it at first; she was so used to all the activity that even now, standing there alone, it seemed to be still going on when it wasn't. She looked at the phone. She still wasn't sure what— But she was tapping out the number quickly now.

"Decker Barnes Pharmaceuticals," a voice said.

"Mr. Henning. I want to talk to Mr. Henning."

I'm the one at your party ... you know, outside ...you said call?

"Mr. Henning's office."

Her eyes were quickly surveying the aisles as she said, "I want to talk to Mr. Henning."

Hurry!

"I'm sorry, he's tied up now. And then he'll be leaving for the day. May I know who's calling?"

She wanted to just hang up but knew it would be a mistake, would be suspicious. So it just came out: "Dorothy Adams."

"Would you care to leave a message?"

"That's all right."

"Can he return your call?"

"I—I'll call him."

Why, she wondered now, had she hung up so quickly? Wrong! Her hand kept the receiver pressed a while longer down on the hook. It was as if she'd been running a million miles. She couldn't see how she'd be able to bring herself to do that again. She was scared again.

Denny was parked a few cars away, by the curb, but as she walked toward him, a woman's voice said, "Ter?" Her sister. She was wearing a long black leather coat, with a gray fur collar of some kind. And a sharply-angled, red beret. "Ter, I want to talk to you. Let's go someplace."

"I got somewhere to go. I can't right now."

"Ter, I want to talk to you."

"I can't I'm tellin' you."

"Ten minutes? Five? You can't give me five minutes?"

"I'm tellin' you I've got to go."

"Then listen to me. Ter, Mom's going crazy. Pop. Can't you go a little easier on them while you're there?"

"What've I done to them? I sleep there, once in a while I eat."

And here it was coming, you could see the change in her face: "You're treating them terribly, you're worrying them! Christ, they got enough on their head! Dad not working—You'd think you'd realize—"

Look who was talking! Screwed half of America, from what she'd heard, and now once she'd married a *certi*fied public accountant, she was *Mrs.* America! And anyway everything was too late. Everything.

"I gotta go."

"Ter."

"I gotta go."

"Then go!" Then yelled after her: "Ever since you were a kid! No one could ever talk to you! Never! I drove here twenty miles!"

Terri whirled, wanted to scream back: "*Me?* What about you? Who could ever talk to you? And big asshole brother!" Instead, she hurried to the car, slammed the door shut. "Get outta here! Get the hell out of here!"

Denny said, after about fifteen minutes of driving in silence through the deepening darkness, "What d'you think my name is?"

"Look, I'm in no mood for jokes. Let's just get there."

"I'm askin' you. What d'you think my name is?"

She looked at him. The way he was staring ahead told her that something was bothering him, and it occurred to her it had started to happen right after she let out all that to him about her sister.

"All right," she said. "Doyle." His name.

"No, it ain't Doyle." He still wasn't looking at her. "It's Wolski. I'm half Polack."

"Yeah?"

"My mother made my old man change it. He was goin' for a job at this big furniture manufacturer's and she'd heard from someone who heard from someone that you had a better chance getting hired there being Irish than Polack."

"Yeah?"

"I think it was a crock of shit. My mother's Irish, you know, and I think she didn't want a Polack name anymore. So the poor son of a bitch changed it. He got the job. But all the shitty jobs he had after that it wouldn't have made any difference if he was a nigger."

"That's something."

"I was sixteen I heard I was half Polack. I heard someone saying. It don't matter to me I'm Polack, but I wish someone told me." A while later he said, "The poor son of a bitch."

But then his mood and hers soon began to change; he slowed up a little, the two of them leaning forward and looking from left to right through the darkness. She said, cautiously, "I'm sure it's on this side," pointing to the left. Then, "Go a little slower."

The headlights spread open the darkness to a sharp curve in the road. They came around it slowly.

"There," she said. "That's it, I'm sure. Yeah, it is it."

If Wyndan had three or four horses, this guy had fifty; the split-rail fence went on like a half mile. Denny stopped the car. The entrance to the estate was a rutted road between two stands of trees. She remembered bumping up and down in the packed car, there must have been seven people in it, some on laps. You couldn't see the house from here, but she remembered exactly where the big van was with all the food, and the two station wagons that pulled up with the musicians. She remembered just about every detail of the kitchen, with the huge island in the middle and all those copper pots and pans hanging down over it. She remembered looking out into one of the hundred other rooms and seeing them in tuxes and gowns, even the little kids. She remembered the smell of garlic on her hands. And him—how could she have ever blanked out on him? *Him?*

She motioned for Denny to drive on. As he did, the rear tires made a little screech. Maybe it was just coincidence, but just then dogs began barking and howling way up there. She didn't remember dogs, but they may have been locked up that night. They drove on, along the fencing. If they couldn't get to him any other way, there could be a hundred dogs, it didn't matter, somehow they'd do him here.

*C*HAPTER NINE

Soon after Rick came in on Monday he called the police in Radnor Township, where Wyndan was murdered. Though he was sure the Philly cop he'd given Takoni's letter to must have "passed it along," as he said he would, that was before the murder and who knew what the hell anyone really did with it?

He said, "Detective Zinn, please."

But Zinn wasn't in, would be back that afternoon. Rick left a message for him to call him back

Afterward, sitting back from his desk, he found himself thinking again of that message yesterday. It was stupid, cruel, it had to be someone who was still blaming the "media" for the Watergate business and everything else rotten in the world. There had been nothing in that column that could have caused this, someone would have had to be absolutely downright crazy— Even so, you couldn't be responsible for crazies.

Still, he was aware that not too deep in him was the hope that the motive was really robbery.

Rick raced to his right, his gloved hand in one fast arc slamming the little hard black ball against the left wall near the far corner, where it angled off with a snap to the front wall, and now to the back where it rebounded to Larry. He rocketed it with a scooping swing and it went to the front wall, then off to the left, then came back in a black streak no more than a foot off the floor. Rick got to it, lunging, hit it even lower to the front wall, where it went crazy in the corner and came back and skittered off the floor a few feet in front of Larry's low, reaching hand.

Rick didn't see that, he'd gone into the right wall after he got to the ball; saw Larry, now, on both knees, how he'd fallen. Larry had his head thrown back; he was gasping. Rick bent over, holding onto his thighs, letting his breathing get easier.

Larry said, "Hell, I didn't know the idea was to win."

Rick laughed. They shook hands and Larry pulled him to the floor. Larry covered City Hall down in Philly, was hardly ever up here during lunch; this was a date they'd had to break several times. Though Larry was very good, Rick knew beating him didn't exactly make him handball champion of the world. Or the gym. There was a kid in his early twenties he could just about beat one out of three. And there were even a few oldtimers, in their sixties, gray hair on their shoulders, who took him to the limit.

One or two old guys, he'd heard—the figure varied—had died right here on the floor. Which is how, some of the others said, they'd like to go.

Back in his office he started to play back Bernie Frank's tape, lowering the volume, making pencilled notes on a yellow pad. He was five columns ahead, which was a little low for him. He had a few other floaty kind of themes in mind—there was a married couple caring for schizophrenic children in their home, there was a woman somewhere who was supposed to do therapy with patients in a swimming pool; he'd like to do some columns on recreation and healing—sailing, for one;

he'd sold his boat when he moved here but would be buying another. And one on mixed marriages, which he'd already done, but this one with a guy in it who was christened, had a bar mitzvah, had one grandmother who made great pasta *fagiole*, another who was known for her *kugel*.

He reached for the phone, at the first ring.

"Mr. Broder?"

"Yes."

"Detective Zinn. You called."

"Yes. And thanks for returning the call." He explained that it was about the Wyndan case and that Joe Cooperman had given him his name. "I got a couple calls and a letter sometime before the murder that you might be interested in. If you've got about five minutes, I'd like to tell you—"

"Look," Zinn cut in, "I've got people hanging on my neck now. And I always prefer in person, anyway. So if you want to come over, you can come over."

Rick was tempted to let the receiver drop from the full length of its cord. If there was ever an angry edge to a voice ... To coin a phrase, he thought, that's a guy with a bug up his ass.

Zinn was a tall man with a long thin neck, made longer by a face that was just as wide. He sat back in his chair as Rick, sitting next to his desk, told him about the column, the calls from Louise and Mary, and the letter from T. Takoni.

"Well, what," said Zinn, arms folded on his chest, "can we do about calls with no last names?"

"I'd say absolutely nothing." This guy was getting to him; it was as if he were tolerating a kindergarten kid. "But I didn't really call about them. I thought ... Takoni ... it might mean something, it might be close to someone's name, someone who works at NCI, was laidoff."

"You say you already gave this to a cop in Philly."

"But that," Rick explained again, "was before the murder. But now, and since it's in this jurisdiction—"

"I see," Zinn said. "Well ... okay. We shall see. I thank you." He nodded and then stood up.

He didn't put out his hand, and Rick thought, Scu-rew you. As Rick was about to leave, Zinn said, "Let me ask you something. Can I ask you something?"

"Why not?"

"You think he was under all that pressure?"

"Who?"

"Whalen?" Zinn said. "Down in Philly."

Oh, Christ. The cop who collapsed one day, then broke down and helped send three other cops to jail. And though he'd been part of the stolen property ring, got a suspended sentence for psychiatric reasons. He'd been just one example Rick had used of the stresses of being a cop. That had been five months ago, at least. And for all this time, this guy ...

"Stresses, my butt," Zinn said. "Someone wants to rat, rat. I'm not condoning anything those guys did. Get that straight. But they get ten to twenty and he gets nothing? He was as nuts as my little toe. You thought you were buying steak, Broder, but you bought baloney."

"I bought what the court said."

"I'm sorry. You bought ba-loney."

"Tell me." Rick stared at him. "Is this why you couldn't give me just five minutes on the phone? Is that it?" Zinn said nothing. "I called you about something that might be nothing, might be something, but you couldn't listen, and you couldn't tell me then, 'Hey, I disagreed with what you wrote.' Or tell me it was full of crap. Or whatever. You had to make me come down here, had to put me through this."

Zinn's eyes narrowed slightly.

Rick, his temper at its edge, knew he'd better just go. But first his finger darted out. "I want you to know I may have bought baloney, Zinn, but I'm not very big at all on taking shit."

Zinn looked as if he was going to leap at him. But after a long, furious stare between them, he grabbed up some papers and walked away.

The following afternoon, at a couple of minutes after twelve, Terri was standing just outside the store, trying to reach a fast decision. She'd been in such a hurry, she'd been thinking all morning about making this call, that she had forgotten to take her jacket. Go back for it? Instead, her hands clutching her arms, she ran to the drugstore next to the corner.

A woman turned to look as she went by. A man turned to look. But for a different reason.

Someone was on the phone, but no one was waiting. Terri stood close-by, her hands still clutching her shivering arms. It was an open phone, but she didn't care. *Just get off!* Once, talking and nodding, he glanced at her, then looked back. *Get off!*

His head was way back now, he was smiling at the ceiling, then he looked down as he rubbed the top of his shoe against his pants leg and examined it. Talking, smiling, listening, talking, turning.

She moved a little closer. The creep, he could smell her perfume! *Mister.* She was almost ready to say it. *Mister, damn you!* She was approaching that now. But then he put the receiver on the hook, stood there thinking, then walked away.

She pushed in a coin.

"Decker Barnes Pharmaceuticals."

"I want to speak to Mr. Henning." All the old, slow stuff. Henning's office now. "I want to speak to Mr. Henning."

"Can I tell him what this is about, please?"

"Can I talk to him? He asked me to call, he knows me."

There was a pause, then, "Who shall I say is calling?"

Christ God, she couldn't think of the name she'd used! And she didn't want to use another one, it might make this woman—she might remember her voice—"Dorothy," she said, "Adams."

"One moment please."

And then a voice that sounded almost like one of those fancy Englishmen: "This is Mr. Henning."

"Mr. Henning." And she turned, her head down, so that her back was facing the rest of the store. "I hope you remember me. I worked at the party you gave at your house last year? And you said if I ever wanted a job, wanted to change jobs, to call you?"

"I'm afraid," he said after a long moment, his voice not the voice that night, "I'm not too clear in my memory on that, Dorothy. And the situation's changed, we're really not hiring now. But if you'd like you can call personnel."

And then he was giving her their number. Didn't remember. Noo, he didn't remember, now that he didn't have a hard-on.

*C*HAPTER TEN

"Lilly."

Miss Schweiman looked up quickly from her desk in the outer office. Mr. Henning, sitting in shirt-sleeves in his office, said with obvious annoyance, "Please screen my calls more carefully."

She felt the blood rising to her face. "I'm sorry, I thought I did. She said she knew you."

"You know," he was saying it almost by rote, "if you don't know someone, ask them what they want. And buzz me first."

"I'm sorry."

"I don't mean to make a big deal. But"—he was returning to some papers on his desk, his temple resting on the fingertips of one hand—"it's been quite a day. Quite a day."

She wasn't angry at him at all; she was angry at herself. She'd been his secretary twenty-nine years and had spent all those years protecting him against annoyances, intrusions, unnecessary work. It was almost physically painful to realize she'd forgotten the most basic rule. She tried to return to her work, but couldn't get her full mind on it. And then she let it all surge through her, what had really made her do it. That slightly trembly, hesitant young voice, that voice and name she remembered from yesterday. And wondering what he'd do when he heard who was calling; if she would see him smiling into the phone, his voice very low; if he would close his door; if he would even leave soon afterward.

Edwin Henning remembered the girl well enough. And he didn't like it. He'd thought of her a few times since the party, though not in months; but he had thought of her: little quick pictures that would come to his mind, mostly when he was trying to fall asleep and which he would dismiss quickly, wouldn't let himself linger on them.

He remembered how he'd stepped outside the house for some air; he'd had two or three martinis, felt good, and there she was over by the trash, looking at him. He had seen her in the kitchen and maybe she thought he followed her out, but he hadn't. And there she was, looking at him and now smiling; not just a smile, a certain kind of smile, a little crooked at one corner. And he'd started sauntering over, but as he remembered it she came most of the way to him.

And it was hello, how are you, isn't it a nice night? Just that, but all at once, though he kept talking to her face and she was smiling back at him, he was thinking: what would happen if I touched those breasts? He wanted to touch those breasts, just touch them, or reach in back and put his palms on that behind, each on a hard cheek and squeeze her to him.

He didn't want to think of it anymore, that he'd even been stupid and lecherous enough to ask her to call him; made himself stop.

"You free, Ed?"

It was his VP for marketing, standing in the doorway, then walking in and taking a chair.

And now that incident was gone, as gone as if it never

happened, and he was immersed again in the problem of their big anti-hypertensive drug they were losing their patent on in three months.

He left for home around seven. His car was parked, like every other employee's, on the large parking lot next to the building. Although he had a houseman who also served as chauffeur when needed, he rarely had him drive here to the office; he was too sensitive to appearances. And most always he drove in in the small Cadillac, though there were three more expensive cars at the farm.

The dogs flew out of their kennel and began barking as he turned into the lane, two Labradors and a Dalmatian: three friendly guys who were all bark. He tossed them around a little, then went in to find that his eldest daughter was there with one of his grandchildren. They hadn't expected him until later, so they had already had dinner. Like most times when he ate alone, he preferred eating at the small table in the kitchen itself. Beautiful, always thoughtful little Nickie came in—"Pop Pop," as though she hadn't seen him before—and sat with him until he finished.

Afterward she went out to the stable with him. He patted several of the horses in passing, but spent a little time with Big Hello. She'd had a problem with one ear, but it was healed now, she was just fine. He turned out the light and they walked back through the white of the floodlights to the house, the dogs around their feet. He let Nickie in first, then walked in and closed the door behind them.

The black Mustang, parked on the shoulder of the road about fifty yards from the lane, pulled away as the barking died.

This had been pure luck. And Denny. They'd come here hoping for *something*, that maybe the dogs wouldn't be barking or that Henning would come driving in or out or maybe even *walk* out. But it was crazy, waiting for just luck.

So they'd driven by slowly, then parked a while a few miles away, then came back and waited again. But it was useless. And this road here, this road was so like Wyndan's to her that it was as if nothing like that could happen twice.

So they'd driven off again, and after driving around it was Denny this time, drawing on a cigarette, his eyes narrowed, who said, "Let's go back once more." And as they came back up the road they saw that car pull into the lane. And she saw something else. From that far away she couldn't see who was in it. But she saw that the driver had to almost stop on the road before he could make the turn.

*C*HAPTER ELEVEN

Dr. Goldstein called Rick the next morning.

Rick said, "Jay, did you happen to see an interview I did with Roy Crane? It was right after his book was published."

"Yeah, I saw it," Goldstein said, "and I read his book." Then, "Pretty good."

Thank yoo, Rick thought. Goldstein had an ego either the size of a Brontosaurus or as fragile as china; you could, Rick felt, give points either way. He was brilliant, was reputed to be an excellent therapist, but he seemed to begrudge every other psychologist or psychiatrist an original thought.

Rick told him about the call he got from Mary and referring her to him, and he asked if Goldstein had ever heard from her.

Goldstein didn't have to think about it. "Yes. Yeah. She called. I'm sorry I didn't get back to you on it, but I never heard from her after that and I put it way on the back burner. But once in a while I think of her. It was a little strange."

"Did she give you her name? Where she lives?"

"No. I don't even think she gave me a first name. Mary. No. She just started talking, she was quite upset. She was worried about her husb—" He checked himself. "You say she told you ... someone in her family? Well, now you know. Her husband. She was worried about her husband. And she was going to try to get him to call me. But he didn't. By the way," he said after a pause, "she's a big, big fan of yours. Said she saves your columns, has a big book of them. And she heard you give a talk."

"She say where?"

"No, just that she heard you give a talk. Oh, and that after you gave her my name and she hung up, she remembered hearing about me before, that you discussed me in your talk, had some very nice things to say about me. So I thank you again."

Rick frowned, but all he said was, "I'd appreciate it if you'd let me know if she or her husband does call."

"Sure. But I sort of doubt it's going to happen—it's what, about a month."

The phone down, Rick sat back and tried to think this out. A few months after he started the column he began getting invitations to give talks—to women's groups, men's groups, church groups, schools. He started accepting them about a year ago, had given about twenty so far, always careful to come across as no more than he was, a journalist reporting on mental health, on "human behavior." And, basically, he'd been giving pretty much the same talk: how he wrote the column, and got the material; how he'd gotten into the field; how he could do this without being a psychiatrist; his most interesting experiences, new therapies. And though he did discuss the work of some of the people he interviewed, he couldn't remember ever talking specifically about Jay Goldstein.

It would have had to be about his specialty, "family violence," as Goldstein referred to it. Rick had talked about such things as child abuse, parent abuse, but he would swear he'd never mentioned that guy by name. And yet he must have; she wouldn't have just made that up. If he could just remember doing it he might be able to recall where it had been. And that might—

Then something came to him full force. Maybe the reason she tried to disguise her voice on the phone was that she had talked to him there.

But at which of the dinners, luncheons, meetings, classes?

Off and on throughout the day, during a pause at the computer or at times between calls, his mind would take a hopeful, new stab at it. But nothing. And toward the end of the day he told himself that's it, forget it. He'd written three columns on obsessions; he didn't need four.

That evening he met one of his oldest buddies for dinner at a crab place in center city. He and Mack, a surgeon, had lived on the same block as kids, gone to high school together, dated together.

Between cracking open a jumbo crab and digging out the meat, Mack asked about Deirdre—she and Rick had gone out a few weeks ago with Mack and his wife.

"Fine. Saw her the other day."

"Is this the one? And I'm getting tired asking you the question."

"Don't be. I might have to trouble you again."

"Come on, she's nice. In fact, too nice for you."

"You come on. I know her two whole months. She wants to be a lawyer—the last thing she wants to do right now is get married again."

"How do you know she doesn't want to get married?"

"I've got a certain feel for those things."

"You're," Mack said, laughing, "so full of crap. Christ, I don't see how you can live like this. Alone. Free to do whatever the hell you want."

They laughed.

Mack asked, "You ever hear anything about Carole?"

"Matter of fact, I heard last week she's married again.

About four months. He's supposed to be a very nice guy. I wish them well."

It was still a little strange, he thought later driving to his apartment, how he could talk about Carole with almost no feeling one way or another. It had been wonderfully right at one time, and then somehow there were two people who didn't seem like the same people who'd married each other. There had been a drifting apart even before the paper folded. But that certainly hadn't helped; he'd been one miserable son of a bitch.

Ever since he was a kid, all he wanted was to be a journalist. And to live on the edge with it. In high school he was the kid who came up with the stories the faculty tried to censor and the kids would picket about. When he'd gone out to Berkeley, he'd been a key pain in the ass on that paper, too. And afterward, after bumming around the country on odd-jobs, and a brief apprenticeship on a weekly, he was the guy on the *Tampa Telegraph* who got the threatening letters ...

Working in PR after that almost drove him nuts the first few months, though it was twice the money. And the offer to come here meant mostly, at the beginning, just being back on a paper. But he came to enjoy what he was doing now. He was good at it, got satisfaction out of it. But he did miss ... the challenge, the excitement of investigative reporting.

And now he wondered—it never hit him until this moment—if *that's* what was really seducing him in this Wyndan thing.

He took the elevator up from the basement garage. It stopped at the ground floor where several people, just two of whom he recognized from the building, got on. One of them, a middle-aged woman, looked at him and clasped a hand to just below her throat.

"Oh, I meant to drop you a note. That article you did on dying at home? That was so beautiful."

"Thank you. I appreciate that."

"I never thought that anything on death I'd think was beautiful. But it made me see— a hospital, no. Be with family, with friends ... If you," she said to the others, while her husband held the door open, "didn't read it, you ought to. You really ought to."

It was a slightly uncomfortable ride the rest of the way, the others not knowing what to say, and Rick had never fully gotten used to this. He nodded goodnight as he got off.

In the apartment, one of the first things he did was turn on the radio to classical music. The thought slipped into his mind that he should call his mother. She was living in Florida— Fort Myers; she'd moved there after his father died, was living with her widowed sister. And was doing beautifully; at seventy-one had even taken up golf. He would call soon.

He played his answering machine but there was nothing on it, just a robotic sales pitch, then sifted through some of the magazines that had come in the mail that morning. Then he went to the refrigerator for a beer, unsnapped it, took a mouthful and a good swallow. He brought it with him to the living room. He started to raise it to his mouth again, then slowly lowered it.

I'm very interested in relaxation techniques. Do you know of any particularly interesting work ..?

He frowned. It had been something like that, from a woman. During a question and answer period. And in answering he'd mentioned Goldstein.

It was weird—how he hadn't been able to think of this all the time he'd been straining to think of it. But only when his mind was free of it—

Goldstein.

Only it had been another Goldstein.

*C*HAPTER TWELVE

She was at the head of the stairs, about to go down, when she heard her mother's voice say in the living room, "Police."

Terri took two quick steps down, then stopped, holding the banister hard. Her mother was saying other things, but all at once that single word had blocked out the sound and meaning of the others. Terri came all the way down, slowly.

"Yes ..." Her mother was on the phone. "What did she say? No. I don't know."

And there was anxiety in her voice.

Terri hadn't intended even hanging around long enough to have coffee, was going to have one standing by the Tastycakes display at the 7-Eleven. But she couldn't make herself move. Her hand couldn't even let go of the railing.

"Yes ..." That's all her mother was saying now. "Yes ... Yes ..."

And there was anxiety even in that.

She looked distraught when she came out to the hall, but even so a touch of surprise showed on her face when she saw Terri by the stairs. She wasn't used to seeing Terri waiting to talk to her; it had to be months since Terri had started a conversation.

Terri said, "Who you talking to?"

"Mrs. Keller called. The Kellers?" He, Terri knew, had been laidoff by NCI, too. "She said the police questioned Mr. Bell. You don't know him, he worked with Daddy. About Mr. Wyndan who was killed? You know he was killed." Terri couldn't even nod, just looked at her. "So they're going to be questioning everyone," her mother said. But she seemed to be saying it as much to herself as to Terri.

Terri went to the closet for her jacket.

"You have breakfast?" But from her mother's face, much of her was still on that call.

"No. I'll get something, I'm late."

"You're not late." Terri was zipping up her jacket. "That warm enough, Ter? It's very cold out."

Terri didn't say anything, wished she would just shut up, shut up, she had so many things on her mind, had to work things out.

"Daddy went out early, he has another interview," like, Terri thought, she was supposed to start dancing.

"I'll see you," Terri said.

Outside, standing on the top step, she felt a little lightheaded for an instant. But just for an instant.

They couldn't wait much longer to do Henning.

They'd been out there half the night, parked off on the shoulder by some trees, spotlighted by the occasional car going in either direction, open for the sudden cop car and the flashlight in their faces. Crazy, absolutely nuts, she'd thought, though she'd whirled angrily at Denny when he suggested twice that maybe they should go.

And even though she was aware now that they had to do someone quick, it was still as if there could be nobody else but that guy up there in that house. It had been enough before, but then to hear his ugly, ugly voice saying: "I'm not too clear in my memory on that ..."

To treat her like dirt, and *I'm not too clear on that.* She had to do him, she really *had* to.

A panic attack hit her a couple of hours later. It seemed to come of itself, without any warning. She was answering a customer's question, her mind wasn't really on it, but she was answering. Then all at once her heart was beating wildly and she was icy and sweaty, and all she wanted to do was run. She tried to fight it, but in complete panic grabbed up her handbag and walked quickly to the ladies' room where she sank onto a covered toilet, her head down in her hands. Her arms, her whole body was trembling as she held her head.

She had to run from here, had to run from here, had to run from everywhere.

"Ter?" One of the girls, right outside the booth. "Terri? You all right?"

"I'm ... all right."

"Mr. Campbell told me to see. He thought you might be sick. You sure?"

"I'm all right. I'll be out."

She could hear her leaving.

The trembling, the slamming of her heart, was gradually easing. But she was so cold. Her blouse under her thin sweater was drenched. She made herself go back.

Mr. Campbell, the assistant manager, a pretty nice guy—the creep wasn't in today—was at the counter. He looked at her, a little concerned. But he said nothing as she returned to her place and put away her handbag, just walked back in the office.

The racing was still in her, but it was as though distant now, small; something she could control. The only time it started to come back was shortly before lunch when a voice said, "Ter?" and she saw Kim, one of the old crowd at high school.

"Heard you were workin' here," Kim said with a big smile. "You look good."

"You do, too."

"You look really good. Hey, I ran into Patty. Have you seen her lately?"

"No." She just wished she would go.

"Well, you ought to. She's pregnant, you know. And she's really big, the baby must be ten pounds, but her face is still small. She tells me they're buying a house. Her husband got a promotion."

She stepped aside as a customer came up, then waited until another came and went.

"Haven't seen you around lately," she said. "You don't go dancin' anymore? You still seeing that fellow, what's his name?"

"I'm still seeing him."

"You don't go dancin' anymore," Kim said.

"I been sorta busy."

Kim, who was holding a large package, said, "Well ... call me sometime. Or I'll call you."

"I'll call you."

"Well ... Take it easy. See you."

"See you."

Terri watched her walk off.

It wasn't that long ago, but it was like a whole world gone.

Her heart was beating hard again, but she wasn't going to lose control. She just hoped that Denny would be outside at lunch. She had to tell him what was happening with the cops.

Edwin Henning had left his office early, grabbing up a few things in his hurry. He'd called his wife because she'd been up half the night, wheezing and pulling in on the inhaler; and though when he called she said she was fine, he could always tell from her voice when something was wrong. And it was only when he kept questioning her that Carrie admitted she had "this slight pain" in her chest.

"Get to the hospital," he ordered. "I'll meet you there."

But almost miraculously to him, they determined that it was just a bad case of indigestion, and late that afternoon he was able to take her home.

With her asthma, her diabetes mostly, he often thought what it would be like with her gone. And it frightened him. With everything he had, it still frightened him. There would be a gap that no one, nothing, could ever close.

Before heading back to the office, he took another look at some of the papers in the briefcase he'd brought with him. It troubled him that though what he had to do was so hard, people who didn't know probably thought it was so easy. Maybe they'd even think it was appropriate that it was being done at night, though the reason was simply that everyone on the committee could make it.

Carrie was downstairs, reading. She lifted her face for a kiss.

He said, "I should be back about eleven. Twelve."

"Good luck, sweetheart."

The dogs crowded together just outside the door, barking and trying to follow him into the car. He pulled away slowly at first, until he was clear of them and they were standing barking behind him, then he stepped a little harder on the gas. A glance at the dashboard clock told him he hadn't given himself enough time. The meeting was called for seven-thirty, which was only fifteen minutes from now.

He did something reckless, something he warned every-one in the family against doing: he didn't stop before pulling out of the lane, just made the turn fast. The road was empty. There were no headlights coming toward him, and none in his rearview mirror. He stepped harder on the gas.

Then he almost slapped himself on the forehead. That one memo! On the chance he might be mistaken he opened his briefcase with one hand as he drove, flipped on the overhead light and began pulling papers onto the passenger seat. But it wasn't there. He slowed up just enough to U-turn, and head back to the house.

CHAPTER THIRTEEN

They had seen the headlight beams spread over the road from the lane, but by the time they jumped out of their car the other car had made the turn, fast. They started to get back in, but stopped; those rear lights were gone.

"This is crazy," he said, out of breath and shaking his head. "This is crazy, this is absolute crazy."

"Whyn't you stay in the car?" Her voice was rising. "I said one of us should stay in the car. You were driving, shoulda stayed in the car!"

"You'n't say anything stay in the car! This is crazy."

"You see who was in it?"

"I don't know. A guy. I don't know."

"A guy," she said, trying to think. "I saw a guy."

"This is crazy," he said.

She didn't want to hear; didn't mind herself saying it, thinking it, knew it was true; but didn't want to hear it.

"Crazy," he said. "Whole thing. I don't know why I—"

"Why you what? Say it!"

"Let's get outta here."

"Why you what? Say it."

"Look," he said. And the way he was saying it, the twenty-two in his hand, his chest pumping, she thought he was going to swing it up to her face.

Let him!

"Look," he said, "you want to do someone? You want to do someone? I'll tell you what! All right. I'll tell you what. I'll go the hell up there and I'll do 'em all—dogs, kids, grandmother, all of 'em, whatever's there." He started to stride toward the lane, but she grabbed his arm.

"Stop it," she said then, forcing her voice lower.

"I'll do 'em all," he repeated, though quietly now.

"Let's just go. Come on, let's go."

And almost the instant they got in the car, before he had a chance to turn on the motor, the lights, they saw headlights coming this way and the lights were starting to slow. The car was going to turn in! She thought she saw a face, just one, started to turn to Denny, to grab the gun from him if he wasn't—

But he was out of the car, was racing over. The other car started to accelerate, to speed past him and curve in there; but Denny was running along with it, two hands on the gun. There was a shot, and the car sped a little farther into the lane, then slammed into a tree. And with the running motor and spinning wheels as background, Denny fired three more times into the car.

He stood there now, just looking; he started to take a few steps away, then came back to look again. And now he was racing back.

She took off the second he leaped in and banged the door shut. She kept her foot hard on the gas until she saw a little intersection ahead, slowed up enough to take it, another country road; gunned it to another intersection, then, taking that, stayed pretty much at the speed limit, thirty-five.

"A guy ... one guy," Denny had gasped as they'd pulled away.

He put the gun, at her instructions, back in her bag. His other one was still in the glove department.

"Use this one," she had said.

Everything the same. So it'd all look a lot more, she'd had to explain again, than just NCI.

"Can't you go any faster?" he said.

"I don't want to go any faster."

Her arms were held out straight to the wheel. The shakes of this morning, this afternoon, were completely gone. You couldn't have the shakes now. She was just tense enough to be alert.

They drove to his place. There without taking off her jacket she pulled open the rollaway bed and lay across it, face down. Here her heart began drumming up at her. Here it was okay.

She felt the mattress give, could tell he was sitting down. He eased down and put his arm around her. She turned and put her arm around him. They just lay there, she with her eyes closed. That's all she wanted; just this. Soon she began to stroke his forearm; but the way she did it, he sensed that this was all she wanted, too. He rubbed her shoulder, then squeezed it hard.

After about fifteen minutes she sat up slowly. "Let's go."

"Where?" He was sitting up too now; looked astonished.

"Let's just go."

He followed her out to the car. She got behind the wheel. She drove some ten miles and pulled into the parking lot of a squat stucco building. Its sign was a glittery GLITTERS.

The place, the dance floor, was fairly crowded for a week-night. Lights twirled through the blasting music on everyone, everything, from the ceiling. A disc jockey was behind his equipment on the large stage—large, for live groups on the weekends.

She took his hand, but he resisted the dance floor.

She tugged at it a little, and he gave. Then he just about stood there looking as first her shoulders, then her hips and legs went with the music. His shoulders began to move too, then his legs. She danced with him into the crowd; they danced around one another; she went part way down in front of him, then up, then danced with her back to him, against him; his hands were on her hips.

Then she waved and her lips said a silent hi to someone she knew whom she'd seen from the edge of the dance floor. His arm rose in response. Hi.

CHAPTER FOURTEEN

Edwin Henning sat slumped against the steering wheel, his head slightly to one side, his face in the bright floodlights stringy with blood. One bullet hole above his left eye, another behind his left ear, one in the ball of his left shoulder. A fourth bullet, in a strange way afflicting the most obscene wound of all, had taken off the tip of his nose.

This part of Chester County, near Unionville, didn't have its own police department and so the call went to the state police. Above the sound of cars pulling up, of doors opening and closing, of voices calling out orders, of the sobbing in front of the dead man's car, was the barking and howling of the dogs standing stiff-legged at the top of the lane.

And almost the moment his identity was known, the cop who first learned it, then the others he passed it on to, seemed dumb struck with the implications: that guy in Montgomery County, that guy Wyndan. Head of a big corporation, too. Was driving his car, too.

But it wasn't until just a little later that someone said, in a further kind of awe-filled way, "Didn't I read Decker Barnes was going to unload a ton of people, too?"

***

The banner head across the *Dispatch* said: SECOND CEO MURDERED.

Rick almost lowered the paper the instant he picked it up outside the door of his apartment.

A sub-head said: STRIKING SIMILARITIES BETWEEN THE TWO KILLINGS, while the headline of an accompanying story asked: WHY DID THESE TWO MEN DIE? And there were photos of Edwin Henning, his car, the main house and, once more, Charles Wyndan.

No one had heard the shots, no one had seen a fleeing car. Henning must have started to come back to the house because he'd either forgotten something or perhaps had wanted to tell his wife something. He was to have attended a meeting that evening which, it was hoped, would finalize the number of employees who were to be laidoff. Unconfirmed estimates placed the number at about eight hundred and sixty. For months, rumors had been running through the company and through Wall Street that massive cuts were coming because their patent on Perezine was running out and the company's potential multi-million dollar new product, an anti-depressant, still hadn't been cleared by the FDA. But the company always denied there would be any layoffs, since they had a "large bedrock" of generic and non-generic drugs According to a recent published report, Henning's annual compensation, including salary, bonuses and stock options, came to $2,740,000.

Although it had not been confirmed yet by tests, a police source said that a bullet recovered in the door on the passenger side seemed to be a .22, the same caliber bullet that had struck down Wyndan. And the accompanying story speculated that the killer didn't necessarily have to be an employee of either company, that it could be the work of an "ideological" assassin or a group of some kind; that it might even be a warning from someone in another company who felt that his job was in jeopardy.

Walking into the lobby of the *Dispatch*, Rick was one of the last people on a crowded elevator.

"What do you think?" one of the advertising people asked him; didn't have to say about what. "A real crazy, eh?"

And someone in back said almost in a whisper to a friend, "Not necessarily."

And a few people turned around and laughed.

The Goldstein he had mentioned at a function, Rick remembered, was Todd Goldstein, not Jay. And recalling what it was in reference to, he knew where. St. Paul's Church, over in Ardmore; a luncheon. There had to have been more than a hundred people there, mostly women. He'd sat on the dais with several women and the priest; the priest and one of the women had handed out awards for various good works. He'd been the main speaker, and in answer to that question about relaxation techniques he had included Todd Goldstein's work in music therapy.

Afterward he must have talked to at least fifteen women clustered in front of the dais, some waiting very patiently for a turn. But which one could have been Mary? Who could he have talked with long enough that she would be afraid a few weeks later that he would recognize her voice? *She says she has a big book of your columns.* Several of the women had said they saved them. He thought he could picture some of their faces, but then again he wasn't sure if they were the faces then or at another talk.

He turned his chair to face his computer and tapped "St. Paul's" onto the screen. He kept a memo of all his contacts at these talks, and two names and telephone numbers were listed under St. Paul: the priest's and Katherine Denson's, the woman who had contacted him and made all the arrangements.

Mrs. Denson, this is Rick Broder and I'm looking for a woman named Mary ...

He looked at his phone, then he swept up the receiver and dialed her number. A young voice, a boy's, answered.

Rick said, "Is Mrs. Denson there?"

"No, she isn't in now."

Rick left his name and phone number, carefully spelling it out. But he had the strong feeling the kid wasn't the best of message takers, and two hours later he called again. This time there was no answer.

About two minutes later his own phone rang.

"Ricky," and the pause.

"Sam. How are you?"

"Ricky, you feel like taking me for a ride?"

Rick frowned. His uncle had told him he was allowed to begin driving again ... And then all at once he was pretty sure he knew: his uncle really wanted to talk about the murders.

This time he made it for after dinner.

His aunt, in her long dress, took his hand in both of hers, smiled up slightly as he bent over to kiss her, then she moved away silently. His uncle sat in a big, darkly tapestried chair, the ex-cop who occasionally worked for him, Wally, on the end of the tapestried sofa. Wally wore an unbuttoned overcoat; a husky man, he sat on the edge of the sofa, his short thick legs apart.

He started to lift himself up but Rick came over and shook his hand.

"I was waiting to see you, son."

Wally had been a lieutenant of detectives in Philly. Rick couldn't help feel a sense of something a little forlorn about these two men sitting in a living room whose lights would never brighten it: his uncle who'd had a busy agency, the lieutenant, a widower, who had won so many commendations. He wondered if they had any work anymore.

Wally said, "You got some uncle here, God bless him. And your aunt. I know a lot of eyes they're gonifs"—he was Irish, but Yiddish had long been a part of his vocabulary—"but your uncle has always been one square guy. Honorable. A *mensch*."

"Wally, what d'you want?" his uncle said.

"I'm just saying. And I'm going to say something else. I always say this—you want something done? Give me one Irishman and one Jew."

"One Jew and twelve Irishmen," his uncle said, smiling around his cigar, and Wally roared. His face was red, he was still smiling as he pushed himself up.

"Well ..." He held out his hand to Rick. "I just wanted to say hello. I had a fine dinner and I just wanted to say hello."

"I'm glad you did. It's good seeing you."

Wally went into the kitchen to say goodbye to the "missus," then touched Sam on the arm and smiled at Rick on his way out.

Sam said, rising from his chair, "Take me for a ride."

Out in the car Rick said, "Where would you like to go?"

"Anywhere. Just drive." But then after only about a half block he said, "This is fine." Rick pulled over to the curb, leaving the motor running so the heat would stay on. Sam reached in under his coat and took out a cigar and matches, and, unable to smoke at home, lit up. He leaned back, drawing in deep, let the smoke out, drew in again, and then let it out again, this time very slowly.

"So," he said. Then, "You talk to your mother?"

"Yesterday. She's doing fine."

"Good. Good. You know something?" he said quietly. "I miss your father."

Rick looked at him. "I do too."

"We hardly saw each other, but I miss him. It was like ... you know, someone's always there? We used to fight like dogs as kids. But you know what? Someone else try to start up with us? We'd kill him. Your father was a fighter."

Rick couldn't think of him as a fighter; even as having much of a temper. His mother and father, two gentle people, were always after him because of *his* temper.

Sam looked at his cigar. He cleared his throat, then said, "Ricky, can I ask you something?"

"Of course. Anything."

"I'm not worried about this at all," he said with a wave of a hand, which probably meant he was really worried. "It's just something that ... happened, it sometimes happens."

Rick waited.

"Last night," Sam said. "I'm watching this fellow on the news I watch every night. Dan Rather. But you know something? I couldn't think of his name all night and half of today. I had to ask Esther."

Rick said, "That's not unusual, that happens to everyone."

"Oh, I'm not worried," he said quickly. "I'm just, you know, talking. But ... it does happen once in a while. Forget a name. Or once in a while I want to go someplace, say, at a certain time and I forget what time. I'm not really worried, I wouldn't bother a doctor with it ..."

No, Rick knew, he was too scared to go to a doctor.

"But I'm just ... talking," Sam said. "I know you're a brain"—he smiled, embarrassed—"and you're in this work."

"Hey, Sam," Rick said, and he put his hand on his uncle's

hand. Sam looked a little surprised. "Uncle Sam—you ain't—you ain't got Alzheimer's."

"Oh, I'm not really worried about that."

"Well, in case you ever are. Let me ask you something. Can I ask you something now? You read, don't you?"

"Of course I read."

"And you know what you're reading."

"I know what I'm reading."

"And you're working. And you hold intelligent conversations—I can swear to *that* one."

"I try to keep up."

"Look, everyone as they get older has little problems remembering things at times. It's normal. Names, so once in a while you don't remember a name—it'll come to you or else just ask. And if you've got an appointment, an errand to go on, write it down, keep a memo pad. Do anything that helps. For instance, there's this guy I know, a young guy, if he has something to do that day and wants to be sure he remembers, he puts his watch on his other wrist. There's nothing to be ashamed about."

"He does that?"

"Let me tell you what just happened to me. I was trying to think of something a guy named Jay Goldstein said and it took me forever until I finally remembered it wasn't Jay, it was Todd."

Sam looked at him. "This happened to you?"

"Yesterday."

"Huh." He seemed to settle back more in the seat. Soon Rick sensed he should let his hand go, and he released it. Sam looked at him. "You're a good fellow, Ricky. A good fellow."

He took a long puff on his cigar. Then after several moments of silence, he said, "So, Ricky," and lifted the cigar again to his mouth.

And Rick, knowing Sam might never get around to asking directly, said, "You read about the murder of that fellow—Henning? It's definite, the same guy killed both of them. One of the reporters told me—the bullets are twenty-twos and so far at least two of them match the ones killed Wyndan."

Sam showed no expression, except for a slight lift of his eyebrows, even when he said, "There's gonna be a lot of worried execs around."

Rick told him then about Zinn making him come to the station to tell him something he could have told him over the phone; then, just as Sam finished muttering "putz," the latest about Mary and trying to reach Katherine Denson.

There was silence. Sam tapped ash into the ashtray, then sat back.

Rick knew there was something else his uncle would never ask. So he said, "Can I call you if I need help?"

Sam frowned sternly. "Ricky," he scolded, "I'm never too busy I can't help you."

CHAPTER FIFTEEN

Terri woke to silence that morning, a silence as she lay there that suddenly became alarming. She sat up in bed, her hand instinctively bringing the blanket up over her bare breasts.

"Den?"

Since she could see all around the room the only place he could be was the bathroom. But there was no answer, and even though the door was open, the light out, she went over to it anyway and looked in. Then she went to the window, but staring as far as she could on either side she still couldn't see his car at the curb.

For some reason her immediate thought was to check her handbag. It lay on the floor by her bed and she unsnapped it, not to see about the money, but the gun. It was there, she had known it by the weight and feel of the bag, but something made her want to actually see it. It was as though this more than anything else, more than money, more even than Denny, was her only protection.

Now, sitting on the edge of the bed, she was suddenly angry at herself to have even thought for a second that Denny had checked out. All she'd had to do, as she was doing now, was look over at the partly open door of his closet where she could see some of his clothes. All she'd had to do was remember that Denny would never check out on her.

The excitement, the tension, that had kept her from falling asleep for a long while was coming back. Denny had had four cans of beer in the refrigerator last night, but she'd only had half of one; he'd finished the rest and then that half. She hadn't needed it to be on a high. She was on that high now, a mixture of excitement, tension and fear. Mostly excitement.

It had to be after nine. She could hear the door to the flower shop opening and closing.

If she ever thought of her job, her home, it was only for a few seconds, and then as things she couldn't be bothered with today: things in her past she'd gone beyond.

Soon she could hear footsteps coming up the stairs, then the turn of the lock. Denny, his face red from the cold, was grinning, a folded newspaper in his hand.

"Babe," he said. Then, taking off his leather jacket and throwing it on a chair, "Man."

He sat on the bed facing her, began opening the paper. Quickly she gestured to put it away.

"Babe," he said, "this is good stuff."

She motioned angrily toward the floor, that they might be able to hear downstairs.

"Babe," he said, a little above a whisper. "Then let me tell you. That guy? That son of a bitch? Oh, what a son of a bitch! You know what? They were just layin' off a million people! A million people. Oh man. Lemme read it to you."

He looked through the paper quickly. She didn't object. Pointing now, he read, "'Henning was on his way to a meeting where they hoped to final—uh, final*ize*—the number of workers to be laidoff. The exact figure isn't known at this time, but it's estimated that it will be more than eight hundred and fifty.'" He lowered the paper. "More'n eight hundred and fifty—and that son of a bitch must be makin' four million a year."

"Lemme see." She wanted to see for herself. Her eyes took in the whole layout—his face, Wyndan's, the car, the house. "Where's it say?"

"Right here." He pointed to the paragraph. She read it, then reread it three or four more times.

"I knew it," Denny was saying. "I'd read about it, I'd heard it."

She was still too busy involved with the story to look up at him. But he was full of crap, she knew; he would have told her. But slowly then, as she put aside the paper, it was as if she had known, too. Had known something. It had been more than that old bastard hitting on her; she could feel it, she knew it. There'd been something—something inside her. Something, the thing in life, that she'd been meant all along to do. That had been put there by God.

Lou Mann got to the radio station at quarter of nine in the morning—the high-in-the-ratings "People Will Talk Station." He stopped long enough to get a container of coffee, then with that in one hand and his briefcase in the other went into his studio. He was on from nine to one; Vic Palmietto was just finishing up, to be followed by five minutes of news.

Lou had brought in two newspapers, though the same papers were delivered here, as well as articles he'd clipped out of some magazines last night, and the answers to a couple of esoteric questions he'd been asked yesterday. Finished now, Palmietto took off his earphones and stood up.

"You don't need guests today," Palmietto said.

"The murders?"

"Brother. Someone let 'em all out of the cage today."

Lou sat at the microphone. Every morning he started off with a few topics he hoped would inspire some calls. But from what Palmietto said, he knew he wouldn't need them. His first call, he saw on the computer screen, was Allen from Northeast Philly.

"You're on the air, Allen."

"Lou, I want to talk about the two murders. They're atrocious acts, of course, but if they're what they seem to be I think they demonstrate that our political leaders and corporate management shouldn't underestimate the frustration and sense of hopelessness of the average working man and woman who give their working lives to a company, and then one day find they're just a disposable chip in the profit game ..."

"Lou, how are you? Something a lot of people aren't aware of is that while a lot of people are getting richer or doing just fine or who've never had it better, there's a lot of us who're really suffering or just about getting along. And when you have people who are thrown out of work and at the same time these companies, their top executives, are becoming richer ..."

"Lou, I think the media should take a good, long look at itself. And they may very well see their own bloody hands. I think the way they've been publicizing CEO salaries has been like kerosene on a fire. I don't remember seeing a word about the dollar value of creativity, experience, of having to be competitive in salaries if these corporations want the best ..."

"Yes, Lou, am I on? I'm going to take a different tack. I know you're going to call this an old chestnut. But I'm telling you, don't be surprised to learn that there's some fine old subversive hands behind this, that it's an attempt to disrupt, to frighten ..."

"I'm a first-time caller but a long-time listener. I own a medium-size business and I've had to farm out some of the work. It's cheaper for me, but it meant laying-off some in-house people. And I may have to layoff some more. And now I'm telling you, what happened to those two ... I'm nowhere that big, but I'm telling you, I feel very uneasy now. I may be getting paranoid, but I don't even know what my foreman is thinking now, let alone some I let go ..."

"Lou, all I want to say is people are mad, they're *mad* ..."

"All I want to say to the previous caller is this is America, buddy. And there are lots and lots of jobs out there. We lose a job, we go looking for another, and in the meantime we count our blessings. And God do we have blessings ..."

"Lou, I'd like to say something to the previous caller—what was his name—Jerry? Jerry, you talk about counting our blessings. I lost a great job and, sure, I've got another job, but it's half the salary. I just want to tell you it sure ain't my blessings that are worrying me ..."

"Yes, Lou. Am I on? I find a strange thing. I'm all for capital punishment—I'm sure you remember me on that. And I always say don't give me that crap about understanding. I hate to say this, but if this is the kind of guy I'm picturing, I really sorta understand ..."

"I'm not for murder, Lou, God knows, but if there ever was a wakeup call in this country ..."

Once in a while Lou would look over at the large glass partition to his left, at his young producer behind it. Sometimes he would roll his eyes at him, sometime throw up a hand, his head way back. Whenever he agreed with callers he let them know. Others he let speak without comment. Still others he let know were idiots, through his usual "you're one heavy thinker."

But today was scary.

Generally the only reason he cut callers off on the seven-second delay was that they said something obscene or maybe mentioned a brand or the name of a store he didn't want on the air. But so far he had to do it five times—each of the calls was just a word away from being a cheer for the murderer. And for future murders.

They left Denny's place when it got dark. Ordinarily Terri couldn't bear being in one room like that for long, but now she almost regretted leaving.

Not that she was worried about walking into the world again. She felt good, strong. It was strange how, where once she hadn't wanted to even look at a story about it, she'd spent hours turning the channels on TV for it, and listening to that talk station. And she wanted to hear even more.

CHAPTER SIXTEEN

As soon as Miss Schweiman pulled into the Decker Barnes parking lot she wondered how she could possibly go into that office. He wasn't dead forty-eight hours. For all she knew he was still in the morgue.

People were pouring into the entrance as though it were any other morning, slowing up to go through the turnstiles, then spreading out across the lobby to the several elevators. And yet from their faces, it really wasn't like any other day. They were solemn; she saw no one speak.

But it wasn't just about his death, she knew. Many of them had to be wondering were they on that list of layoffs. Or even wondering if the killer could be someone in this building; one of them.

The elevator stayed silent as people drifted out onto various floors. She and the two executives going to the seventeenth floor nodded at each other. The door to the executive suite was unlocked. She opened it, to the view of her desk and just beyond it the open door to his office. His desk had a touch of golden sunlight on it, the black leather chair half-turned as though he had just gotten up. The police, she knew, had been all through it, though there was no sign of it now.

The detective who had come to her apartment yesterday to question her had brought a couple of things they'd taken from it—a notebook and a legal pad with names and notations on them she had been able to identify or confirm. And she spoke of Mr. Henning from her heart—the best boss, the nicest person ...

Melanie, from the next office, was standing in the doorway now. "I just want to see how you are," she said.

Miss Schweiman, sitting at her desk, simply lifted her hands.

"I know, there's no words," Melanie said. "Dreadful. Dreadful." Then she walked off.

Miss Schweiman wondered what to do. Carrie Henning herself had called her at home and said, "Please go in, dear, take care of things," as if he was still alive or it was essential to his memory that she maintain continuity.

She started to go through some papers, then frowned abruptly. That young woman, that girl—the nervous voice. She had forgotten about her, though now that she remembered she didn't have to look in her book to know her name. Dorothy Adams. Yes. She recalled Mr. Henning's reaction. Upset. A little too upset, maybe.

But whoever killed Mr. Henning and Mr. Wyndan, she assured herself, couldn't be just some young girl. That call must have been about some nonsense, which is what had upset him, with him so busy. All she'd be doing if she mentioned it was start a scandal. Destroy his reputation and hurt poor Carrie.

Rick was finding it hard to fully concentrate on what Mrs. Carew was saying.

Several people had contacted him about her, claiming she'd healed pets that their vets weren't able to heal, by a laying on of hands. He'd called her, just to talk a bit on the phone, but she said the only way she could really convey it was in person. And here she was, a kindly-looking woman in her sixties, who didn't know how it "worked" except that she'd been very successful, especially with such things as arthritis, intestinal diseases, even some tumors.

Rick didn't promise he would use it, though he would try; he had written about psychic phenomena before, something which always brought in a lot of mail, pro and con, but he'd always been able to fit it into the spectrum of everyday human psychology. This one was fascinating, and he'd see.

After she left he labeled the tape and put it on the shelf with the others he would get to. He had a little more work to do on school phobia, wanted to add a few things to it; but as he brought it up on the screen his mind kept going over to the phone.

Katharine Denson still hadn't called. There was every chance Mary wasn't the real name. And even if he located her what were the odds against her husband having anything to do with this? And—the big question right now—what could he even say to Mrs. Denson? Nothing that he told himself he would tell her really made sense. But he had to call her.

Somehow, as always happened to him in his street reporting days, the right words would come. He had faith in coming through in an emergency.

He tapped out her number, then reached for a pad. A part of having faith. The phone rang once, twice, then a third time. He held on for a fourth ring, and this time a woman answered, out of breath.

He said, "Mrs. Denson?"

"Yes, but would you hold on a second? I just came up from the basement."

"I'm sorry. Should I call back?"

"No, no." She paused, then, "Who's this?"

"This is Rick Broder, Mrs. Denson. From the *Dispatch*?"

"Mr. *Broder*? Oh, how are you? How nice to hear from you. You know something? People still come up to me once in a while to say what a nice program it was, what a nice talk you gave. Tell me, what can I do for you?"

"Well, I hope you can help me. I'm trying to follow through on something and I need some help."

He explained that he'd met a woman at the luncheon he remembered only as Mary and he was trying to get in touch with her. Would Mrs. Denson be able to help him out with some names?

"Mary," she repeated. "I'm sure ... I know ... we have quite a few. Let's see. Does the name Mary Brindle ring a bell?"

"Mary Brindle," he said. After a few moments, "I'm a little embarrassed. But I'm not sure, I don't know."

"She works over at the Budwell Library?" she said. "You know the library?"

"Yes. Of course."

"Let's see, who else. You remember what she looked like?"

He looked toward the ceiling, then said the most noncommittal thing he could think of. "I'd say she was middle-aged. Nice looking. I can't remember her hair ... I feel a little foolish."

"No, you shouldn't. There were so many women there. Look, offhand I can't think of anyone else, at least any last names. Do you need it right away? Can I get back to you?"

"Oh sure. I really appreciate this. I hate to put you to this kind of trouble."

"It's no trouble. I only hope I can be of help."

Hanging up, he tried to get his mind back on work. The first thing he had to do was return two calls. But one number was busy, and as he was about to call the other he thought: No, that one could wait, he'd be on it an hour. He grabbed his coat off the hanger, walked out to his car.

Budwell was only fifteen minutes away. He parked on the street, near the front door. The library was a two-story, fortress-looking building. He walked through the first floor, looking at the women behind the counter and a couple of women who were putting books on the shelves, but no face looked familiar. He went upstairs. There was a woman at the only desk, in a corner of the large room, but he had never seen her before, either.

He came downstairs, wondered whom to ask. He decided on a teenage-looking girl pushing a cart of books. "Miss, excuse me. Is Mrs. Brindle here today?"

"No, she isn't. But she'll be in tomorrow."

"Thanks."

He started to walk off when she called, "Sir?" Then, when he turned, "Did you say *Mrs.* Brindle?"

"Yes."

"Are you sure you have the right one? She's not married."

Denny drove Terri past her house twice, each time slowing up to see if their green Dodge was in the driveway. It was.

Terri knew her mother generally worked today, but either she wasn't going in or was going in late. She didn't want her mother there; her father, she didn't give two damns where he was.

The third time, the Dodge was gone.

Terri unlocked the door and walked into the house. It was cave-like in its silence, its emptiness. She looked in the living room, though, then the kitchen to see if he was there. No. And though she didn't go into his room she could tell in the silence of her own room that he was gone, too.

She pulled out her suitcase from the closet and began putting things in, at first carefully, not wanting to wrinkle her several mini-skirts and blouses, then began throwing in her jeans, all this other crap. She was very careful with her box of costume jewelry; tucked in her high heels, threw her sneaks on top; forgot, then remembered her toiletries, and went downstairs and pulled out from a kitchen closet a number of plastic bags.

In the kitchen, before going up to finish, she wrote out a note which she left on the dining room table: *Have found my own place. Will be in touch. T.*

Upstairs again, she finished packing. The suitcase closed, she held it for several long moments on the bed, though she was anxious to get going. She must have had some good times here, she wouldn't have this little hollowness in her otherwise, but she couldn't remember any of them. And she didn't even know if there were any. All she remembered was the yelling, the screaming, him at her, him at her mother.

She walked quickly downstairs.

His screaming at her. "Bum, you're a bum ... No brains, don't you have any brains? Who thinks like you? Who's got a head thinks like you? I don't know anyone thinks like you! Never be anyone! Never!"

She closed the door behind her. Hard. And walked fast to the car. She was someone, she was someone, buddy, right now! You should only know!

CHAPTER SEVENTEEN

When she woke the next morning Denny was in his jock-eys, standing in the kitchenette next to the bathroom. She'd wakened twice during the night, once so exhilarated it had been hard to fall back to sleep, the second time in concern she addressed now: "How much money you got?"

"I don't know." He didn't look at her. "Why?"

"You don't know what you got? I'm askin'. How much money you got?"

"I—I'm not sure."

"Well, *nearly* how much?"

"A hundred. Hundred anna quarter."

"Where do you keep it?"

He pointed to a bureau drawer, then to his pants thrown over a chair. "How much you got?"

She didn't answer; instead started to get dressed. He said, "You mean I tell you, you don't tell me?"

"I'll tell you when I know. I'm going to find out for sure."

He brought instant coffee over to a card table near the window, then went over to the TV. "I didn't want to turn it on, you were sleepin'."

But he couldn't find news, so he turned on the radio. It

was already tuned to the talk station. Someone, a woman, was saying, "People have no loyalty to employers any more, to their jobs, and no one can blame them. Their employers don't have any loyalty to them ..."

"Lou, I'm the wife of a cop. And I can't believe what I'm hearing. The hatred!"

"Can I change the subject, Lou? I want to talk about taxes ..."

And Terri, sitting facing the radio, her coffee going cold, felt a sudden twist of disappointment.

But the next two callers came back to the subject.

Denny stopped at a store and brought three papers, two locals, one Philly, out to the car. She was a little surprised the story didn't take up quite as much space. But it was still big on the front pages.

She scanned two of them quickly, as if anything important would leap up at her. Then just as she was finishing she heard the sound of ripping: Denny was tearing out one of the stories.

"What're you doing?"

"What d'you mean what I'm doin'?"

"Don't do that! Throw 'em away."

"Why? Tell me why."

"Just do it! Don't *save* 'em, for Christ sake. That's like yelling it from the roof." He still seemed to be questioning her. She started to grab the paper from him, but he grabbed it back. "Throw them away," she said. "Just throw 'em away."

He took all three over to a trash basket at the corner; she watched him stuff them in. It really didn't make all that much sense, she knew; not with them walking around with two guns and a million bullets. But she'd read it somewhere, that that's what a lot of people do, save things; and it's those things ...

Back in the car Denny said, "You said you wanted to go someplace. Where do you want to go?"

"Wilson's."

"Wilson's? What're you going to do there?"

"What am I going to do there? They owe me money. And I left a scarf there."

"Babe, you think ..?"

"I want my money. And I want my scarf."

She'd thought of this when she woke up concerned last night. And somehow it was the scarf that nibbled at her the most. She would get the money, if she had to break their necks she'd get it, but that scarf. It was her favorite, and there were so many thieves there, and if anything would kill her it would be someone there—any other place but there—stealing her scarf.

He pulled up to the entrance.

"I'll be right out."

He watched her walk off, in those thin high heels and tight jeans, and her hands in her jacket pockets.

He couldn't remember ever seeing her so high—high in this kind of way, anyway—even with grass, beer, or both together; even that time she'd had more than a quart of beer and a shot of Calvert's and was just about walking on the ceiling before she got sick.

She walked through one of the cash register aisles without looking to either side. Betty had taken over for her at the counter. Betty, a nice black lady, was the only one she'd ever gone to lunch with. She looked shocked now.

Terri said, "Bet, you see my scarf any—"

But she saw it herself now, under the counter to the left. And when she looked toward the office the creep was looking at her and just starting to stand up. She went to his doorway.

"I hope," he said, "you don't think you can continue working here."

"I came in for my money. It's a week and three days."

"You'll be getting it. Whatever's owed to you will be mailed to you."

"I want it now."

"I'm sorry, I can't give it to you now. You know I don't make out the checks. And you were out one day, I don't know—"

"It's a week and three days. I want my money."

"I can't give it to you, Terri."

"I'm not leaving 'til I get it. I'm going out of town today. I need it. And it's mine."

"You just tell me where to mail it."

She walked into his office, closed the door.

"What're you doing?" he said. He was standing next to his desk.

"I want my money." Her voice was low, but all her rage at him was compressed in its menace.

"I can't give it to you. I don't make out the checks."

"I'm not leaving without my money." *Don't*, her eyes said, *fuck with me.*

"Terri, I don't want to threaten you, but you're trespassing. You don't work here anymore, you're trespassing. I don't want to do anything—"

"All I'm asking for is my money. You've got the records, you know when I was in."

"Terri, you're trespassing."

"I want my money!" Her voice had become loud.

He reached over to the phone, began jabbing at it. She didn't care who he was calling, it was her money!

He was standing there now, phone to his ear, apparently hearing it ring; looking at her. Then he put it down, sat at his desk, began looking through a small pile of sheets, and then wrote out a check.

Betty still looked in shock as Terri came out. Terri lifted a palm, to say goodbye, and Betty nodded.

Terri walked out. She never felt so powerful, invincible.

And it was the same at the bank, her next stop. The teller, whom she'd never seen before, seemed to take it personally that she was taking every penny out; and then, when it came to cashing her paycheck, said she couldn't do it. As Terri began raising her voice, she went over to the manager. When she came back she went immediately to the cash drawer. Altogether, $949.75. And all at once she felt free, wasn't bound to that room, even to this city.

First, though, she wanted to go to a mall, get some new things, maybe some new perfume.

She'd always loved malls, from the time her mother first took her to one as a kid, then through the years to all those times she and the girls used to go and walk, sometimes run, in laughing groups through the corridors and stop to have samples of real, real expensive perfume sprayed on the back of their hands or to "ooh" or say something like "oh no, gross" to each other's purchases. And there'd been that one mall, gone now, that used to have a merry-go-round right in the center of the first floor, where they'd hop up with the mothers holding their kids, only to go around standing by the horses, wanting but feeling it would be dumb-looking as teen-agers to sit on them, and anyway the main thing was knowing guys would inevitably be drawn there and would wait for them to come hopping off.

They drove now out to a mall on Route 1, which wasn't the closest one but a big part of this great feeling of freedom was being able to just get in a car and ride on a sunny day like this with nothing else to do. The parking lot was only partly filled and most of the people inside were either a million years old or mothers pushing strollers. The long bright corridor the entrance opened up to seemed to offer an invitation to come running through.

She stopped first for perfume and decided on "Charlie,"

with an atomizer, because she had liked it on one of the girls at work. Earrings, she really didn't need any more earrings, but several in a window farther along were tempting, and she and Denny went in and she bought a pair that Denny also liked— very long, with silver links and a turquoise pendant. And a little later, though she hadn't expected to buy these zip-on, over-the-knee black suede boots today, she would have even if Denny didn't grin and nod as she modeled them in front of his chair. Then a Western shop—as soon as she saw a certain embossed cowboy boot in the window she knew she had to get them for Denny, his were almost without heels. That, and for herself a denim shirt with cowboy boots printed across the front.

She hated to ruin any part of the day with food shopping, but they'd have to do it eventually, so afterward she had Denny stop at a supermarket where she bought a half pound of sliced baloney, a half pound of ham, a packet of American cheese, a big bag of potato chips, another of pretzels, a few cans of Campbell soup, hoagie rolls, then some detergent and paper towels.

It was only at the checkout counter, after she'd paid, that her fingers quickly counted the bills in her wallet that were left. She was a little startled to find she was down to a little more than seven hundred dollars. But now as Denny hoisted the bags, it was beginning to go out of her mind again. She, Denny, money, would go on forever.

Driving to work, Miss Schweiman decided she would tell the police. Actually she had pretty much made up her mind the night before. It had been while she was reminiscing again about Mr. Henning, Carrie, their children; how she'd always been treated as, really, a part of the family.

But for the first time in a long while she had let herself

feel some of the tiny stings of jealousy she had occasionally felt then. And she'd been trying to assure herself ever since that she really wouldn't be doing this to hurt them because she was sure now it couldn't be that. She loved them all.

Katherine Denson called shortly before noon to tell Rick that she'd managed to dig up a list—an incomplete list—of the people who'd attended the luncheon, and she had four more names for him, one a Maryanne. "But I only have a telephone number and address for two of them, Mary DeCarmo and Maryanne Alman. Do either of them sound familiar?"

"I'm embarrassed to say I don't remember."

After he jotted them down, she gave him the other two. "I don't know them," she explained, "and I haven't been able to find out where they live. They're apparently not members of the church. You see, you didn't have to be a member to go to the luncheon. People brought guests. And there were people who bought tickets as they would for any charity."

Rick's immediate impulse when he hung up was to lift the phone again and begin calling. But this one he had to give a lot of thought to. *Mrs. DeCarmo, Mrs. Alman, this is Rick Broder. Did we meet at the luncheon? Yes? Did you call me a few weeks later ..?* Right, he could just picture her coming right out and admitting it. A woman who had disguised her voice.

If he could only find out more about them. If one of them was married to someone who'd worked for NCI or Decker Barnes ...

It would also mean locating the other two, perhaps talking to neighbors, storekeepers. Things he'd done as a reporter and done pretty damn well. Time-consuming things, but that was what he'd been paid for, was all he had to do.

He lifted the phone quickly.

"Broder's Investigations."

"Sam. Rick."

Silence, then solemnly, "Yes, Ricky."

"Sam, you said I could call on you if I needed any help. I need some help."

"All right."

"But I want to say something now. I want to pay. Your regular rates."

"I take it back. Not all right."

"Sam. Why?"

"My regular rates are too low."

Rick laughed. "Well, whatever."

"For a smart boy, a boy with so many brains," Sam said, "you can talk pretty foolish. Now what is it?"

Rick told him, Sam interrupting a few times to have him spell the names. "I can't always hear so well on the phone," he said, apparently remembering.

Rick called Deirdre from the office at quarter to six. "It's the devil calling," he said. "Can you take any time off to go out for dinner? Bring Beckie?"

"Devil? You're an angel. I'm going nuts. Something's got to go—the job, school or the kid. I think I'll keep the kid. She'll love you, I'll tell her you asked, but she's got exams tomorrow and she's with a friend."

"So what time? Six-thirty? Seven? Eight?"

"All three. I gotta get out of here. But nowhere where I have to dress."

"Well, bring shoes. You might have to run."

"I'll see you," she laughed.

As he was walking out Joe Cooperman called to him from his desk. "Hey, you're in the right field, Rick, there are more crazies in this world than roaches. The city desk just got a call there's some graffiti on a billboard near the Schuylkill Expressway about the murders. A photographer is on his way there now. The guy didn't say what it says, he's probably the same guy that sprayed it."

Rick drove with Deirdre to see it. The billboard, under curve-necked bright lights, said: DECKER BARNES, and below it, on an angle, was a cough drop box spilling out lozenges.

And across it, in large, red spray paint, was: GO .22!!

They sat parked, staring at it. Her hand soon found his. And when he turned to her she was looking at him, her face etched with the same dismay. Forgetting about everything else—those poor victims, their families—didn't the idiot know it might not just be "them" now, but *anyone,* next?

*C*HAPTER *E*IGHTEEN

The picture of the billboard took up almost half the front page of the Philadelphia *Sun*, a tabloid. Denny grabbed one off the pile, then gathered up another Philly paper and the *Dispatch*. In the car he stared at the picture, quickly looked inside for other pictures, then flipped through the pages of the other papers. He went back to the *Sun* fast, the only one that had it.

He couldn't look at it enough, then put it on the passenger seat so he could glance over at it while he was driving. He almost ached with wanting to show it to people. He wished he could wave it right in the faces of all of them over at Quick Man Lube. He wished he could show it to his mother's Old Man; wished he could tell all the guys, his old buddies—Eddie who was going to spend his whole life tarring roofs; Tony who couldn't wait to show him his Harley, screaming it in circles under his window; even Mike who got it into his head somewhere he wanted to learn to be an accountant.

And what a great movie it would make. He tried to think of titles, something with .22 in it. He could see the action—first Wyndan, then Henning. And then someone else, a lot of someone else's. He wondered who could play him, who Terri. He could see Tom Cruise; there was another one, but he couldn't think of his name right now. And Terri? Madonna? But Terri was prettier than Madonna. Prettier than all of them.

He could see the beginning, he could see all the action. But he never thought to give it an ending. It didn't have an ending.

As soon as Terri came out of the bathroom from the shower, tucking in a corner of the towel near her left arm, she knew from Denny's curved little smile that he had some kind of good news.

"Hey," he said, and handed her the paper, picture up.

She took it in both hands and sat down with it. She looked up, unable to digest it right away, then looked at it again.

This was *them*.

GO .22!!–this was *them*.

It was more them than anything else that had been said in the paper, anything on the radio, the TV. It was like they were *inside* .22, a part of it.

And way up on a billboard.

Someone had climbed up there, he could have broken his neck, someone had climbed up there and sprayed it, spraying up for the straight lines, around for the curves. Even made a circle for the dot in front of .22.

Denny said, grinning, "Let's go see it." He seemed to be jumping up and down, though he was pretty much standing still. "Okay?" he asked.

"Is it in the other papers?"

"No. Maybe they'll get it in later."

Terri opened the paper, partly to try to be cool—it was the greatest thing you could be; and partly—mostly—to read it. She'd come to want to read everything about it. And she saw something now that tightened her a little, about four paragraphs into the story. It wasn't written up as anything big, was mentioned as just one of several things police were doing. They were, she read, "interested in talking to a woman named Dorothy Adams, probably a young woman, who called him at his office the day before he was killed. The call seemed to have upset him ..."

"Read this." She was pointing to it.

Moments later he was looking at her in alarm. "This—the name you ..?" Then, "Where'd you get the name?"

"Made it up, what d'you think? What d'you look so worried about?"

"I'm not worried, I'm just askin'."

"Keep it down," she said, motioning at the floor.

"I'm not worried," he said again, his voice lower. "I'm just ... askin'."

"It's just a name."

He still looked a little concerned, though. But later, after he came out of the bathroom, his face broke into a big grin.

Don't save anything, she'd said. But there, held to the refrigerator door by a magnet, was the picture of the billboard.

They were getting dressed to go out when the phone rang. Denny stopped in the middle of pulling on a sock and picked it up. "Hello," he said, and then his face immediately changed expression. He began jabbing a finger toward the phone, his mouth saying that it was her mother.

She waved furiously, shaking her head.

"No, she isn't," he was saying. "No ... No. Yes, I did hear from her. Yesterday. She sounded fine ... No, she didn't say where .... No ... Yes, I will. I promise. I'll tell her." Setting back the phone he said, "Wants you to call her. You oughta, I guess. She'll be sendin' out the police."

Terri finished dressing, pulling on tight green knit pants,

a green-striped knit top; put on peds and then worked her feet into heels. While Denny was finishing, she went over to the window and pulled aside the curtain and looked down at the street. The call was trying to bring her down. And that was something even seeing the name in the paper didn't do. In fact, it had heightened her sense of high.

She should leave town. But for some reason it seemed impossible. She didn't know what, but it was like ... she still had things to do here.

Rick was at his computer, answering mail, when he got his first call of the morning. "Rick. Lou Mann. How's it going?"

"Good. How's it going with you?" He'd been on Lou's show twice. "And what're you doing calling me now? Isn't this showtime?"

"Who says no? I got to make this quick. I'm still getting calls on those murders. That shrink you interviewed about layoffs, violence—what's his name?"

"Crane, Roy Crane." He gave him his phone number and address.

"Goodbye. Why do you always call me when I'm working?"

Rick smiled and put the receiver down. He turned back to his computer, started to read what he'd written, then slowly sat back fully in the chair.

I talked with you on the radio. One of the women at the luncheon at St. Paul's who said she saved his columns. So she had talked to him twice before she called here: at the luncheon and, sometime before that, on the radio. He tried to squeeze out a face from his memory. A face from all those faces. And soon one began to form.

CHAPTER NINETEEN

I cut out your columns, she'd said. And then something like: *I bet I have most of them.*

He remembered another woman in the cluster, breaking in to say something to him—he thought she was the one whose son wanted to go into journalism—and then after she was finished, the first woman saying, "The only things I used to cut out of the paper were recipes." Sometimes, she'd said, people have a problem they think nobody else has, and it's so good when you read you're not alone, what other people do about it, what the biggest psychiatrists do.

So many people said that to him, but now that he had her in this context he could remember her saying it, too. And then about the Lou Mann show. She was the one he was sure said she'd waited almost two hours to get through to him. He remembered the great warmth of her goodbye, her clasping his hand in both of hers, and that smile. A tall, thin woman, who looked to be in her late fifties, with a high cheek-boned face and frizzled graying hair, she reminded him, now that he was thinking of it, of some of those photos of tired-looking women in Appalachia back in the Depression. Only she was nicely dressed, as he remembered. And the smile had bright-

ened that face. He searched his memory for a name, if she'd
given him a name, but after several minutes he gave up.

He started to make a fast call to Katherine Denson, to see
if the description would help. But she'd wonder, she would
have to wonder, why he first didn't simply call Mary DeCarmo,
Maryanne Alman.

Instead, he called his uncle.

Denny shrugged it made no difference to him when she
said she wanted to drive. She gunned the motor before pulling
away, enjoying the roar and vibration. She got the first sniff
of grass before she reached the corner, and now Denny was
leaning over to her with the joint. She shook her head; it was
always an upper for her and she couldn't get much more up
than she was now. She wouldn't *want* to get more up.

"Where we goin'?"

She didn't know; she didn't care. All she'd wanted was to get
out of that room, now to get past all these creeps, to open up.

He said, grinning, "Hey," drawing it out. She'd cut out,
around and in, the Toyota's horn blowing behind them now
on the two-lane shopping street. And Denny hadn't said it to
caution her. She started to take another car, then changed her
mind and pulled back in. It wasn't any thought of police that
did it, she just wanted to do something else.

Something was drawing her to her old neighborhood.

It wasn't the house, it wasn't her parents; she wouldn't go
if she thought she would see them. She would skip that street.
It was ... just something to do.

From here, in Upper Darby, it was about eight miles to
Dowlyn.

He said, "Where you goin'?"

"Just cruising."

He put on the radio to a rock station, then, remembering, went to talk; but someone was talking about some other shit. He switched to rock again, was slapping at his thighs now.

"Hey," he said after a while, realizing from this intersection, the diagonal of a McDonald's and a Texaco station, where they were heading; were almost there now.

"Just feel like looking at some shit," she said.

They were on the main shopping street; it was only about four blocks long, included a state liquor store, a bar, a movie theater, Turner's over there, a pizza parlor, a lawyer's storefront, an osteopath's storefront, a laundromat, mini-market, the fire company around the corner. Christmas, the volunteers would drive Santa around on top of the hook and ladder, its siren going and horns blaring. July Fourth, it carried waiting lines of kids through the maze of streets, after the parade was over.

There was St. Francis Elementary, adjoined to the taller church on a hillock. Oh shit, she thought, *that's* what scared me until I wised up? She looked at faces they passed, two of which she recognized; it was as if she was looking at them from a height. She turned into a street that led to the park. If it was supposed to evoke any feelings, it didn't; it was something dead, gone. And it was the same looking over at Patty's house, then Joanie's and Molly's.

But it wasn't the same thinking of what was up this next street. She turned into it, then drew over to the curb. Right ahead, taking up three or four average lots, was a three-story stone house, with a circular drive and what she knew was a pool among the trees in back.

There was only one other house on this block, equally grand, though not as large. The second one belonged to Old Man Dowlyn. His family founded the whole place; the community was proud of them, proud that some of them still lived here.

But the bigger house—people could never figure them out. Him, at least. That's where the Devores used to live. Her friend Robin.

A lot of people around here wondered why he wanted to live here, why he'd had Old Man Dowlyn build him this place when they could live somewhere fancy, like the Main Line or Chestnut Hill. Nobody ever did figure it out, though maybe it was like someone said, "He just likes it here."

She'd been in that house a million times to play with Robin, had been in their pool, had been in all the rooms—a poolroom, even, and a room with a cabinet filled with rifles and shotguns and with deer heads all over; and Robin's room, all silky-like. And here she'd come with her mother that day, for Mr. Devore to drive her to the Poconos.

A big man, with a shiny face and clean-smelling aftershave. The first father—the first father and mother—she ever knew who played tennis and skied. And they were always kissing each other and the kids, hello, goodbye, I'm home now.

And the first person outside of a teacher she remembered asking her questions like, "Are you interested in going to college? What subjects do you like?" Things she couldn't always answer, and she'd squirm inside, and he'd change the subject. And it wasn't just on the ride up to the lake, but sometimes when he'd see her alone; or like that time he took down a racket from a closet and showed her how to grip it in front of a long mirror.

But then one day there was Robin not looking at her, never looking at her anymore, then word coming back from Patty, then lots of kids, that she'd been found screwing Tommy in the park. And, "Oh, are they mad at you. Oh, are they mad." And Robin changing schools, and that same year their moving away ...

Denny said, "What's the matter?"

She'd been only half aware that she was staring down, that her fingers were picking at each other. "Nothing."

It wasn't only Robin she hated all these years. She hated Robin's mother, her brother, but she hated that father most of all. *What subjects do you like best, dear? You don't know how much we're looking forward to having you, dear.*

And even the memory of his aftershave. She was staring at the house again.

*C*HAPTER TWENTY

The security guard, looking troubled, gave Rick the news as he walked into the lobby in the morning. Someone had just heard over the radio that four more spray-painted GO 22!!s had appeared overnight—two in Philly, the other two in different suburbs.

"Is this a crazy world?" Harry said. "Tell me, is this a crazy world?"

Rick went directly to the newsroom. Joe Cooperman wasn't in, but he got the details from another reporter, Ken Lowell. The graffiti in Philly had been sprayed on billboards, while the others were on the walls and doors of two manufacturing plants. The two in Philly looked to be exact duplicates of the first one. But the colors and spraying of the others were different, even from each other.

"So the way it looks," he said, "one guy's done all the ones in Philly, and now we've got two other kindly souls out there."

Rick said, "We're running the pictures this time?" The paper had decided to hold off using the first one, thinking it would be too inflammatory.

"You kidding? Now we'd be the only paper that didn't."

Rick was in his office only about five minutes when Lowell

showed up in the doorway. His face said there was further news. "Thought you'd like to know." Reports were coming in of corporate execs beefing up security, not only for themselves but their families. "But that's not all of it."

A story had just come in over the wire, from Cincinnati. Someone had sprayed across the entrance of an electrical appliance manufacturing plant: Come HERE .22!!

Wally called later that day, just to confirm the spelling of Maryanne Alman's last name. But before he hung up he said, "You happen to listen to any of these talk shows lately?"

"No."

"God," he said, "*people*. Most people, thank God, have their heads on right, but you should hear some of 'em. It's like this murderer is George Washington or something."

Rick was tempted to ask him how he and his uncle were making out. But he held back, though it was hard to. And the following evening, early, Wally called again.

"The boss," he said, "wants to know can we come over."

His uncle had never been to his place before, though Rick had asked several times. He came in now, in a long overcoat and a black Greek sailor's cap, and stood just past the foyer, looking around the living room. He nodded several times.

"Very nice." It would, again, be a while before he got around to the point.

"It's very nice," Wally echoed. But from a glance he gave Rick, he seemed anxious to get on with what they'd come for.

Rick said, "Give me your coats."

Sam shook his head that he was okay. Curious, he went over to the picture window and looked out at the light-dotted blackness below. "Very nice. This got one bedroom? Two?"

"Two." Rick explained he used one as an office.

"You own it? Rent?"

"I rent it."

"Surprised it ain't gone condo yet."

After turning down something to drink, they sat on different ends of the sofa, in their coats, Sam with a cigar out, unlit, and Wally with a little notebook he drew from his inside jacket pocket. He opened it between his knees, leaning forward, seemed about to read from it, but then said to Rick, "We did some checking on all the subjects. Got a little so far. Two seem clear, two're could-be's. Now this," he explained, "is going by whether their husbands have been laidoff the last few months."

He referred to his notebook. "Going by that, Mary DeCarmo—no, she's a widow. And Alman, Maryanne Alman, no—husband's his own boss, a plumber. But these other two ... One's a Mary Englehart, the other Mary McKenzie. Both husbands have been been laidoff within the past few months, though McKenzie I understand just got a new job."

Rick said, "Either of them work for NCI? Or Decker Barnes?"

"Haven't been able to find that out yet," Wally said as Sam continued to just look on. "The boss feels you know what she looks like, let's go with this. We know where the women live and where they work, and I agree with the boss that the best and quickest way you might get a look at them is at work."

"Where do they work?"

"This Englehart lady's at Norden's—the toy place? McKenzie's at O.L. Stein's. Supposed to be in costume jewelry. Norden's is open tonight, we checked. Stein's isn't. So that's really why we came over. So if you'd like ..."

"I'm ready," Rick said, and with that Sam looked at Wally and slowly pushed himself up to his feet.

Rick drove, with Wally in front and Sam smoking in back.

Norden's was about a fifteen-minute drive, toward Philly on the Main Line. The store took up half a block, with parking on two sides. There was a sprinkling of cars.

"Look, really," Sam said to Rick, as though just thinking this, "there's no use all of us. You know what she looks like."

Only two of the checkout aisles were open, and it took just a glance to see she wasn't at either of them. He spoke to a young black man at one of the registers. "Do you know if Mrs. Englehart's working this evening?"

"Yes. She's ..." He motioned in the general direction of five aisles, then turned to check out a customer.

Rick wandered through the aisles, looking even at obvious customers, then at a woman in a green blazer with a name tag. She wasn't the one, he realized as he came closer, but he looked at her tag anyway. Nell G. He headed back up an aisle he'd already covered. And toward the front was another woman wearing a blazer. No, it wasn't her, either. But her tag did say Mary E.

"So if you want," Wally said to him, back in the car, "we'll do Stein's with you tomorrow."

And then from Sam: "I'll talk to you first, Ricky. You'll decide."

Sam called him at eight in the morning. "Pick me up," he said. It wasn't: do you want me along?

Rick wondered why. Why he'd said last night, "You'll decide." And then he thought he knew. It had been to put off Wally. He just wanted to be alone with him. And the fact was, it felt good being alone with Sam.

Sam said, soon after they left his house, "I was thinking something. I was thinking maybe you don't like me calling you Ricky."

Ricky looked over at him. "Why would I mind?"

"You're a grown man. You're an important man."

"Sam. Come on."

"I was just thinking. I remembered I never liked anyone calling me Sammy. I had more fights ..." A little later he said, "I was thinking something else. Your father was always the bright one. He was a smart boy, a smart man. He was good in school he was this high. Me, since I was this high I was a *grober*. Rough, tough. Your grandmother, she heard I was in Golden Gloves, oh boy. But she was right, it wasn't for me. I was terrible in a ring, but you could always bet on me in an alley." He stopped, then asked, "You mind ... I'm talking?"

"You kidding? I love it. I enjoy it."

"Let me ask you. Your father and mother—did you ever think of going into their business? Being a druggist? Not that you should have, with your ability."

"No, I never did." What he didn't say was that he'd barely been able to wait to get far from here. And sometimes it was still a little hard to believe he was back.

"I don't think your dad, at least, wanted you to," Sam said. "My boys, they didn't want this business, and truthfully it was just as well, they weren't right for it anyway ...Why I'm saying, why I'm talking," he said, and he seemed a little embarrassed, "is I've been thinking. You know, we're in like, you, me, we're in like the same business in a way. I mean the psychology business. This business, you always have to be one step ahead of the next person. You always have to use your wits. And you try to do good. And if you've got to hurt someone you want to try to be sure it's someone who should be hurt."

Rick reached over and squeezed his arm. "That's a real compliment, Sam."

"I'm ... you know, just talking." He looked a little flustered, then all at once bent forward slightly, looking around. "I think ... I think," he said slowly, "this is it."

He meant the street that led to the large shopping center over which the eight-story department store, O.L. Stein, towered.

The two of them walked in together. They entered through the lingerie department, were passing racks of blouses now, then after looking around Rick got directions from a saleswoman. But the only person at the costume jewelry counter was a young woman in her twenties.

"Let's just walk around," Sam said.

It could be that Mary McKenzie had never been in that department or had been transferred. Rick asked a saleswoman inspecting the labels on coats if she knew her. "No," she said, frowning, "I'm afraid I don't."

They headed back. And as they came out of the men's department they saw that a woman had joined the other clerk at costume jewelry. Rick didn't have to go closer to know who she was. Tall, graying, high cheekbones.

CHAPTER TWENTY-ONE

If Rick just took the cutoff ahead it would take him to Mary McKenzie's neighborhood. And a part of him, as he passed the intersection and headed back to the office, saw himself turning and doing it.

But Sam and Wally, or maybe just Wally, would be there soon. Or maybe they were there already, this time with just one person to ask about, a guy named McKenzie who had a job now, but where did he used to ..? He told himself it still wouldn't necessarily rule McKenzie out if it wasn't NCI or Decker Barnes.

At the office he found more than a half dozen messages waiting for him, some requiring a call, others in reply to his calls.

The first time the phone rang his hand flew to it.

But he didn't let it happen after that. He made calls, got calls, went out to lunch with his boss, the features editor, where the talk was about everything but work. He started a new column right after he came back, was checking some of his notes when the phone rang.

He had the feeling this was it, but then remembered he'd had something of this feeling almost every other time the phone rang. But it was it. "Ricky." It was Sam.

And the pause, this time, wasn't long. McKenzie had been laidoff from NCI.

It kept coming back, even though Terri tried. There were too many other things, they had to cool it, had to figure things out, what to do, maybe where they should go. But it kept coming back, like right in the middle of a ride or yesterday while they were out looking at those Honda bikes, Denny running his hand over them and looking at her with a smile.

But it was hardest to push away at night. Like tonight.

Robin begins screwing at twelve—could have started at *five*, for all she knew—begins screwing at twelve, maybe she'd even been still eleven, and here who gets blamed?

Did anyone ever tell you you're funny? That's something else Robin's father had said on the ride, after he'd laughed at something she said which she didn't even know was funny. And it happened several times after that, there and at home, where he'd laugh at something she said and she didn't know why, but she'd smile or laugh because he was laughing. She had thought at the time it meant he thought she was bright; it made her happy; she even tried thinking of funny things to say.

It never hit her he was making fun of her, of the way she spoke or thought or something; there wasn't any clue to that. It never hit her until she was aware they weren't letting Robin be friends with her anymore; and for sure that time he drove right by her in that gray Mercedes and she knew he saw her but then made a slight turn of his head.

Her heart hammering, she put her arm across Denny's shoulder; he was lying naked, his back to her nakedness. He stirred slightly in his sleep, then touched her wrist, then his hand reached back and found the hair between her legs. She didn't want that, but didn't move. His hand soon drifted away.

She felt herself gradually calming. She mustn't do anything. But the thought that calmed her was that that man, that zillionaire, might be dead, or suffering.

She just wanted to find out, she told herself in the morning, what happened to them after they moved away, where they lived. She'd resisted doing this until now.

His first name was Walter, she knew; his wife—Terri remembered thinking she was pretty but not as pretty as her own mother—his wife never called him Walt, always Walter. Walter Devore.

There was no phone book around, so she called Information but then suddenly realized she didn't know where to ask her to look. She had her try Philly first. Meanwhile, she was aware of Denny standing next to her.

He said, "I'm just going for a little ride, I'll be right back."

She hated being left here without a car, but the operator was back on, so she motioned for him to just go.

"I'm sorry, there's no listing for the name."

Where else? Blindly: "How about Bryn Mawr?"

"I'm sorry," the answer came, "there's no listing there, either."

Denny just felt like getting out a while. Mostly it was because he was sure she wasn't telling him the truth. He knew she wanted to do Devore, but all she said were things like, "I just want to see what happened to them ..." Denny eased up on the gas. He was suddenly going too fast even for him, on this street.

He loved being .22—it was exciting seeing those pictures, seeing it in the headlines. He liked thinking of it as him being a 2 and her being a 2.

But so far, he told himself, it was all her. He had people he wanted to do, if they were ever going to do anyone else. There was the manager over at the Lube, and the guy, the Jew probably, who owned all of them. There was his former boss at Huttle Trees, or the boss his father used to talk about who promised to make him foreman at the warehouse but when his father had to be operated on for his back gave it to some dago. Or some of the heads he saw each day in the paper, on the back pages under Business, guys that everyone else on the sidelines, cheering, was afraid to touch.

Terri, he was thinking more and more, was crazy. But at the same time that he thought this, it scared him. He meant really crazy, not crazy meaning having an adventure, fun. This was the kind of crazy where everything was gone and they took you away. It scared him thinking he would lose her, that he would never see her again. That he would go through some kind of long, long life without ever seeing her.

He turned at the first street he could, and headed back.

She said when he got back, "Where were you?"

"Ridin'. Cruisin'."

"Let's get out of here."

In the car, as they started off, she said, "Let's go to Turner's for lunch, okay?"

There were several people in the luncheonette, all adults. Tash, behind the counter, waved, and Sonia who was scraping off the grill looked back over her shoulder and smiled. "How you doing, honey?"

Denny decided on a hoagie. Terri wasn't hungry at all—she couldn't remember the last time she was really hungry—and decided that maybe the easiest thing to get down was lettuce and tomato on white.

Sonia, coming over to take their order, frowned as she was writing it down. "You know something, honey? You got skinny, you should eat. You're skinnier'n the last time you were in."

Later, paying the check at the register, the place almost empty, Terri said to Sonia, "You ever hear anything about Patty?"

"Oh. The baby's supposed to be any second, that's all I know. You know it was born yet?"

Terri shook her head. "What about Joanie?" she asked.

"Oh, I don't remember the last time I heard about her."

Terri asked about a few other of the girls, then said, "You remember that kid Robin? She used to come in here a lot, we were kids? Robin Devore?"

Sonia thought, made a face, shook her head. "Don't remember her."

"I think she lived in that big house on Cedar. Remember those people?"

Tash, drying his hands on a towel looped to the counter, looked over at Sonia. "You knew them. I just read his company took over the Stacy."

Terri looked at him, then said as though in surprise, "You know something? I don't mean her, I got her mixed up with someone else."

Terri said quickly, "Right here," which meant "park here." There was a phone at the corner, near a small sign CASINO BUSES. A group of elderly people were standing there, waiting to board for Atlantic City.

She said, next to the phone, "You got change?"

He went into his pockets, came out with just two nickels and some pennies. She gave him a dollar and he went over to a little store whose signs said they sold newspapers, periodicals, cigarettes and lottery tickets.

The Stacy, everyone knew the Stacy: an old, high-class hotel in Philly. She got the number from Information.

"The Stacy."

"Mr. Devore," ready to hang up if she was put through.

"Is he a guest?"

"Doesn't he own it?"

"I really don't know. I only know we're owned by the Sanderson Company."

Terri hung up, got their number; also in Philly.

"If you're on a touchtone phone," a recorded voice said, "press One if you know ..." She finally reached a human voice. "Is Mr. Devore there?"

"No, he's away. Would you like to leave a message?"

She was about to say no, when the instant it flared into her mind it just came out: "I'm an old friend of his daughter's. Robin. You know where I can reach her?"

"I'm afraid not." Then, "You say you're an old friend?"

"Yes."

"Well ... all I do know is she goes to Penn."

*C*HAPTER TWENTY-TWO

Rick parked in the crowded lot, near the entrance to O.L. Stein's. They would be closing at six; it was quarter of. People were swarming out into the cold darkness, as though a warning whistle had gone off, many carrying O.L. Stein shopping bags in gloved hands. He was one of the few to go in.

He wished he could remember what she'd called him about on the radio. He'd been invited on for the usual, to talk about his work, what subjects seemed to be the most popular, his experiences, the work of some of the people he'd interviewed. And there must have been fifteen, sixteen calls.

He watched her from the far end of the aisle. She was shifting between two customers, each of whom took her to a different section of the counter. One was walking away now. The other was holding an earring up to her ear, looked at a small mirror, shifting her head around. She handed it back, prowled some more, asked for another. She went to the same mirror, and through the same motions with it. Then, pressing both earrings against her earlobes, she was questioning Mrs. McKenzie about them. Soon Mrs. McKenzie was ringing it up and handing her a little white O.L. Stein package.

Rick walked over. She was putting some of the other earrings back into the counter. When she looked up and saw him her face was pleasant, as if he were any other customer, then a look of surprise came over it.

He said, "Hi."

"Hello." But it wasn't just surprise anymore; she seemed a little startled, uneasy.

"I'm Rick Broder. We met at St. Paul's?"

"Yes, I know. I'm ... surprised you remember me."

"Why wouldn't I remember you? You didn't exactly insult me—you said you save some of my columns. You called me on the Lou Mann show."

There was just a flicker of a smile. But the uneasiness was still there, had even deepened.

He said, "How've you been?"

"All right. Fine."

"I'd love to talk to you. Would you have a little time when you close up?"

"I—I'm sorry I won't be able to. I've got to go over a few things, then I have to go home right away."

"It doesn't have to be right now." Then, just a little more forcefully, "I would like to talk to you."

She stared at him, as though trying to read into his eyes. "I'll ... call you," she said. "I'll try to call you tomorrow."

"Great. I'll look forward to it."

He didn't expect the call. From her reaction, she had to suspect that, especially after the murders, he was trying to pin down that muffled voice, pleading for the name of a psychiatrist for "someone" in her family. Why else would she seem so tense?

But the call did come through. Only about a half hour after he came into the office.

She didn't say hello, didn't say his name; just a hesitant, "This is Mrs. McKenzie."

"Good morning. How are you?"

But she didn't seem to hear. "I do want to see you," she said, almost in a monotone. "I want to talk to you."

They arranged to meet in an hour and a half at a restaurant in the same shopping center as O. L. Stein's. He got there several minutes early. The place was almost empty, since it was after breakfast and before lunch. He took a booth toward the back. When she came in, standing uncertainly in front, he went over to her.

They ordered coffee, she with a quick shake of her head when the waiter asked if she would like anything else.

Rick said, "Are you sure?"

"Yes." She looked distracted.

Rick, trying to ease the way, said, "Have you been working at Stein's long?"

"No, actually just the past five days. Up until then I worked two days a week for a podiatrist."

"It sounds like quite a change."

"I enjoy this very much. You see more people. It's nice."

"Were there," he smiled, "any particular types of feet you miss?"

She looked at him, bewildered. Then she smiled for the first time, saying, "I was out in the waiting room. I didn't see all that many."

"I thought that might have been one of the perks."

She smiled again. Even in that gaunt face he thought he saw something of the young woman years ago. Attractive.

He said, "You know?—I've been trying to remember. I'm just curious. When I was on the Lou Mann show. I've been trying to remember which was your call."

"Oh, I called just to get something off my chest, not particularly to get any single answer. And I used the name Doris," she said apologetically, "because, you know, I didn't want neighbors linking it to my family." She stopped, then it seemed to burst out: "I called just to say my family is an example of where you have a couple of children who aren't a problem, and then there's one, in our case a daughter, who's been raised exactly the same way but has always been a problem."

"I remember very well now," Rick said.

"You were very kind. I knew you'd be very kind." Tears started to show in her eyes. "I told you, I save your columns. So many of them—it's like you're writing about me, like that's what happened to me or my sister or when I was a kid or in my marriage. And they're also very educational. I mean, I finished high school, but I didn't have a chance to ... better myself. I still don't read many books—I read magazines. But what I was saying, I read your stuff, I save a lot of 'em ... in a scrapbook. I'm even gonna need a new scrapbook. And I get my kids sore because whenever you write something that really hits me or I think can be important to them, I read it to them. Anyway, I want you to know, whenever your stuff's in the paper yours is the first thing I go to."

"That's very kind of you."

"Well, it's true."

Rick said, "Can I ask you? Did your daughter ever see a therapist?" He remembered giving her a few names, off the air.

"No. I tried talking to her about it, but she wouldn't hear— Look, it's not like she's done something *criminal*. At least nothing I know about. But I'm afraid."

"You don't have to answer this at all, but is she on drugs?"

"I don't think so. I know she was, she did everything, but I can almost swear she's not on drugs. But what I'm saying is—it's hard to explain—she's like always angry. She don't talk to us for days, weeks, then you try to say something she screams.

With my husband mostly. I tell myself maybe it's because she was a late baby, like we gave our best to the first two, we didn't really ... plan her. I tell myself we oughta've moved out of the neighborhood. She had girlfriends, they were just like her, though she was always the leader. But they worked out fine. Patty, she's married, having a baby, may even had the baby. There's Joanie ... I hear she's going to college. There's Molly ... she's married, has this nice card shop, I understand, in Chestnut Hill. But Terri, I'm afraid for her. She's still seeing the wrong boys. I just heard she quit another job. You say one thing to her she doesn't like, or she gets something in her head— I'm afraid for her."

She lowered her head, clasping her hands. Rick said nothing. If he'd learned any one thing from the experts it was don't talk simply to hear yourself talk; don't say you understand when there's no way you can really understand. Just be there, let the person know you are someone they can unburden to.

She lifted her head. "Whew," she said quietly. She dried her eyes.

Rick said, "Can I ask you something else?"

"Of course."

"Why didn't your husband get in touch with Dr. Goldstein? Or did he see someone else?"

Mrs. McKenzie seemed to have forgotten, or was hoping Rick had forgotten, the call she'd made to him at the office. "I'm very embarrassed."

"Don't be. Please. Please don't."

"I mean ... I tried to disguise my voice. And I might as well confess it all, I was going to use another name there too, but I froze and it came out Mary." She hesitated, then drew in a breath. "The reason I didn't call back ... he just wouldn't go. It ... was dreadful, there was a point I was afraid he would do something to all of us, but then one day it was like ... like after a storm. It all went away. And then he began just sitting by the TV, smoking, that's all he did was smoke and watch TV and go out and get beer. Then ..." Once again she paused. "The police," she said. "The police talked to him. He'd worked ... you know, NCI? I don't know you know, they've been talking to just about everyone laidoff from there. And that was it, he says they even shook his hand ... I'll tell you, Mr. Broder. I've never told anyone this, but I can tell you. I'd thought—a part of me thought— that maybe he'd gone crazy and slipped out of the house and ... and actually did it. But thank God. He's even found himself another job. It don't pay near what the other one paid, but things could be good. Things could be good if only ... Ter ..."

He said, "Mrs. McKenzie, I wish there's some way I could help."

"You gave me a doctor ... I don't know what more," she said, shaking her head.

"Does she live with you?"

"God. She lived away, then she came back home, then ... she just left again. No goodbye, just a note. And I haven't heard from her. I called her boyfriend and he said she wasn't there, didn't know where she was, but I don't know ... You know," she said, "what I'm sitting here thinking? If she would talk to you. If I could get her to talk to you ... even just two minutes on the phone. Maybe then all of us could go see someone, a family therapist. If she would, maybe my husband would."

"From what you say, I doubt she'd want to talk to me. But I'd be happy to for whatever it's worth."

"I don't even know where she lives." Mrs. McKenzie drew in a long breath. "I don't know why I'm unloading on you like this. I— Yes, I do," she said then, looking at him. "I know why. You make it easy. And I thank you." She reached out and squeezed his hand. He squeezed back.

Outside, walking away, she turned once to wave a little goodbye. He felt so sorry for her, she was such a nice, good person, he felt a little guilty for what he was thinking. He was sure she'd told him everything—with just one possible exception.

Had she been so tense and uncomfortable with him at first because she was embarrassed about having disguised her voice? It could be. But it might also be that, though the police may have cleared her husband, they didn't know what had brought on her call to him—that he'd threatened to kill his "boss," his "bosses."

CHAPTER TWENTY-THREE

Terri and Denny drove into Philly early that same afternoon. Terri, driving, couldn't remember the last time she'd been in the center of the city, though she'd driven by it last year to see a rock concert down at the Spectrum, and once to see a Flyers game. She could see the skyline ahead, a few of the buildings skyscraper-high, two or three with a bluish tint in the cold sunlight; and among them, the sight of the statue of Billy Penn staring out above City Hall.

Devore was still not in, and Denny had said, "We're not just going to sit around here, are we? Let's take a ride."

Which had been what she was thinking even before he said it. She couldn't handle being in that room any more. She wasn't even sure she should be driving. She was on the edge of that line between being anxious and panic, but she didn't want to tell Denny you drive. Especially once she'd started. And it was getting worse, she was starting to sweat now that the traffic was thickening. She knew approximately where Devore's building was—she'd gotten instructions from one of the voices on the phone.

I have an appointment and can you tell me where ...

Not that she was going up there, she just wanted to see the building.

But it was getting worse. All the people along the sidewalks and crossing at corners or diagonally across the street, and a siren somewhere, and all the horns.

This was it, this building had to be it. And he was on the twelfth floor, she'd learned.

She circled the block and then headed in a direction away from center city, on Walnut Street. She knew the stadium was out that way, she remembered being able to see it from the bridge on Walnut that went over the Schuylkill. And if she could get to the stadium ...

There it was.

After crossing the river, she made the first left turn she could. But here was the huge brick stadium and she still didn't know where she was.

He said, "Where you goin'? What're we doin'?"

"I want to find Penn."

She made several turns, then at a red light saw the kids first—all the kids walking along the sidewalks carrying bookbags, or lined up in front of Chinese food vendors, or jogging in thick sweat suits, or resting on their bikes waiting for the light to change. And she could see some of the buildings, all matching red brick, and kids walking through an archway. She searched faces, hoped by some miracle she would see her. But the light turned. After about a half block she had to stop. "You drive." She was almost out of breath, felt as if she'd been running.

So that's where she went. That's where the little bitch went.

They drove to Atlantic City, though she didn't particularly want to go there. She just wanted to do something. But even as she stepped on the boardwalk she wanted to be back in the car, to keep driving somewhere else, anywhere; was too jumpy to be any one place. But she mustn't let Denny know.

She walked with him in the biting wind, then they took

refuge just inside the Trump Taj Mahal. He said, "Maybe we could get in," even though he knew they'd ID you if you didn't look twenty-one. She didn't say anything, sure he wouldn't try; he wouldn't want to be turned away, in front of her. And he didn't try.

She said, "It's too cold out, let's go back."

He drove. She sat with her head back, and though she closed her eyes a few times she couldn't sleep. Most of the time she just stared as the evening deepened into night around their headlight beams.

Soon after they came off the Walt Whitman Bridge he made a series of turns which she knew wouldn't take them in the direction of his place. After about fifteen minutes he slowed up.

She had no feeling at all about what she was looking at. But she knew from a sound that came from his throat that he was disappointed. GO .22!! had been scrubbed off.

Denny couldn't find parking anywhere on the block in front of his apartment. As they came around the corner she saw her mother standing under a street lamp by her own car, looking toward the door to Denny's place. Terri grabbed Denny's arm; he turned to follow her away, but at that moment:

"Ter. Terri." Then, "Terri, please." Her mother was walking up to her. Her heavy cloth coat hung partly open. "Ter, I want to talk to you. Let me talk to you." Terri just stared at her. "Ter, please. Please come home."

Terri, still holding Denny by the arm, started walking to his car. Her mother took hold of her arm, but instead her hand closed around the shoulder strap of her handbag. The bag fell to the ground. Her mother bent down and picked it up. And just moments later, before grabbing it away from her mother, Terri saw her staring at her in horror.

*C*HAPTER TWENTY-FOUR

Mrs. McKenzie called him about four the next day.

"Mr. Broder, this is Mary McKenzie." She sounded distressed. "Am I calling you at a wrong time?"

"No, not at all."

"I–I don't know why I'm doing this to you but you've been so nice and I don't know where else to turn. And I'm going crazy. I haven't even told my husband this, he would go crazy. But I can't keep it to myself anymore, and I trust you not to tell anyone."

He waited.

"Mr. Broder." But then she paused. And then it just came out, her voice trembling: "She has a gun. Terri."

He said, "How do you know?"

"I was waiting for her. Last night. Outside her boyfriend's place—I don't know for sure if she lives there, too. I wanted to talk ..." Still another long pause. "I don't know if I'm doing right. I don't want to hurt her. I don't want her hurt."

"Tell me how you found out."

"I– Like I said, I was waiting. And I saw them coming, her and that ... that fellow. And I wanted to talk to her but she ... turned away. I reached out ... for her arm, I reached for her arm, but her handbag came off. And when I picked it up I felt it."

"You mean from the outside?"

"Yes. It's one of those—it was a soft bag. And I felt something hard in it. My hand went around it. I know, I know what it was."

"Did you ask her why she has it?"

"She just walked away! She wouldn't talk."

"Do you know if she ever had a gun before?"

"Not that I know of."

"Or belongs to a gun club? Goes to a shooting range?"

"I never heard. I don't know what to do. I'm afraid to tell the police, I'm afraid not to tell them. I don't want to hurt her. Like I told you, she's never done anything like ... like *real* bad. But I don't know what to do."

"Why can't you tell your husband?"

"I'm afraid. They're like fire and oil. It'd be a war, they're liable to kill each other."

"Do you mean that? Are you really afraid of that?"

"I don't know what I mean. But I'm afraid, yes. They both have tempers. But what— I'm sorry, I'm so sorry, I'm pouring it on you."

"I did say I'd like to try to help, didn't I?"

"You want to know the truth? I'm afraid of losing her. I keep telling myself maybe things will be all right one day, things will work out. And the gun—I don't want Terri to think I'm accusing her of ... of anything, I don't want to ruin it forever."

"Do you think you might want to make another try at just talking to her?"

"I— You know, I told you I'd called. I don't know if she was there, but she never called back. That's why I went over. But as I say, I don't know for sure she even lives there."

Rick said, "Where is this place?"

"It's either in Upper Darby or near it. I don't know the

exact address, but I know it's on Millway near Banner. Above a flower shop. I've even blanked out on his last name. Denny, but right now I can't think of his last name."

"You know," Rick said, "you might be getting yourself all worked up over nothing. A lot of people carry guns these days. I myself don't like it, but they feel they need it for protection."

There was still another pause, then, "You know? I'm so worried about her, I never really thought of that. I mean, I thought of it, but—but the way she's been lately, particularly lately, I kept only thinking bad things. But it could be that, couldn't it? I'm still scared of it, I *hate* guns, God knows I hate guns, but it could be, couldn't it?"

Yes, it could be, Rick was thinking afterward. But certain things kept nagging at him. A father laidoff by NCI. A father who rants about killing bosses and seems violent or deranged enough that his wife calls for help. A problem daughter. A problem daughter going with "the wrong boys." A problem daughter going with the wrong boys who has a gun. A problem daughter going with the wrong boys who has a gun and hears her father ranting about killing bosses. And a mother who, finding out about the gun, might not be thinking of those two murders but can only think of bad scenarios for that daughter.

But what about Edwin Henning at Decker Barnes? How could that fit in?

There was no point in even trying to speculate now. The first thing was to try to learn something more about her. And if the gun she owned was a .22.

Rick was getting ready to leave a short while later when he suddenly thought of the names of Terri's friends that her mother had mentioned yesterday. Three first names—Patty, Joan, Molly.

He hadn't even thought of them when talking to her. And he didn't have their last names. One of them, he recalled, had a store somewhere. But what kind and where? Of all the friends, she might be the only one he could conceivably talk to tonight.

He was lifting his jacket off the hanger when he saw Joe Cooperman coming into the newsroom. Cooperman grinned at him broadly from his desk and raised a thumb. Rick went out to him.

"The son of a bitch hit again," Cooperman said. "Didn't kill anyone this time and he got away, but they've ID'd the bastard."

Rick was now one of several people who stood at Cooperman's desk to hear. About an hour ago Peter Domen, chairman of the board of Domen Tools, was walking from his house to get something from his wife's car when someone rushed out of the bushes and shot at him, missing. Domen wrestled with him and was struck on the head with the butt of the gun before the guy, with Domen's daughter-in-law screaming from the doorway, broke free and raced away in his own car.

"He's one lucky son of a bitch, Domen," Cooperman said. "You'd think he'd've had himself surrounded by bodyguards, the dumb bastard, with all the talk about them moving the plant to South Carolina."

Rick said, "They find the gun? The bullet?"

"Didn't say. And they haven't named the guy but I hear he used to work there."

"It could be a copycat thing," someone said.

"Yeah," Cooperman agreed. "The cops aren't ruling it out, but that's not what's really coming from them."

Walking to his car, Rick had to caution himself: don't start cooling it yet about the girl, her father. Not a disturbed girl with a gun, whose father had been laidoff from NCI. Not even a father she apparently hated.

But there was nothing to do about it this evening anyway, unless he wanted to go to the cops with something her mother had shared with him in such good faith. And no way would he do this yet.

He sat for several moments letting the motor warm up. He pulled out of the lot, then had to stop at the first corner for a red light, a long light. And as he was sitting there, it just rose up in his mind.

A card shop. In Chestnut Hill.

*C*HAPTER TWENTY-FIVE

A half hour later Rick was driving through street-lamp illuminated Germantown Avenue in the Chestnut Hill section of the city. It was the business artery through the "Hill," as many of the wealthy, old-line Philadelphians who made up a good part of its citizenry referred to it.

He drove slowly along the cobbled, trolley track-striped street, glancing to either side. A bookshop; antiques; art galleries; a little hotel; a few small restaurants. Some of the shops were darkened for the night.

He saw, ahead, what looked to be a card shop, and it was, but as he pulled to the curb next to it he saw with a sag of disappointment that it was dimly lighted for overnight.

He continued on, driving up the full length of the avenue, to where it entered Montgomery County, then he came around the block and headed back, this time cutting into side streets. And about a mile down, near the intersection of Germantown Avenue, he saw a sign on an open shop, WE'RE CARDS.

An elderly woman was rearranging cards; a young woman with blond bangs and long earrings was sitting near the cash register reading a catalogue.

Rick said, "Would you happen to be Molly?"

The young woman's eyes brightened. "Yes." She stood up.

Rick introduced himself, said that Mrs. McKenzie had mentioned her name to him. His name didn't seem to mean anything to her, but Mrs. McKenzie's brought a smile.

"Oh, how is she?"

"She seems fine."

"Gosh, I've got to give her a call one of these days, it's been so long."

Rick said that he was trying to locate Terri and that Mrs. McKenzie thought she might know.

"She doesn't know?" she said. "Geez. What a shame. No, I don't know where Terri's living, what she's doing—we haven't been in touch with each other for about a year."

"You were good friends, I understand."

"Like this." She put two fingers of one hand together. "I don't know what happened. And it isn't just me, there's a couple other friends—did Mrs. McKenzie mention Joan? Patty?"

"Yes."

"We were a real foursome. Since we were kids. They don't hear from her any more, either. It's been a long time."

"And you don't know why?"

"I can only guess about myself. We had ... a little quarrel. It was stupid, over a little dress, who should be able to buy the dress, who saw it first. But we always had, like, little quarrels—you know *girls*—but they never meant anything. This time, though, she didn't call me even when I called her, she never called me back. And I felt, you know— You know what I really think?" she said. "Because I got married. And I think it's true of Patty, too. As for Joanie, she's going to college. What I'm saying is, I think it was sorta like we left her behind. I don't know."

"Well, maybe when she gets married ..."

"I have a hard time seeing that. At least not for a long time. I don't think she has the temperament. She used to be, maybe still is, so much fun. And crazy. I mean, crazy fun. Do things. If she made up her mind to do something ..." She didn't finish, just shook her head with a smile. "I should try to find out where she is," she scolded herself lightly. "I should. And I will."

"Her mother is very unhappy what's happened. I don't know what it is, but Terri refuses to talk to her, see her."

"That's sad. I think of the two, her mother and father, she loved her mother. I know it. But she used to get real angry at her because her mother always ended up letting him have his way."

"What kind of guy is he?"

"When I knew him? I thought he was a nice guy, a real nice guy. It's funny, you grow up," she said. "When we were kids nobody liked their father, everyone liked the other guy's father. It's funny."

"How was she in school?"

Molly smiled. "Like all of us." Holding out a hand, she turned it from side to side. So-so. "But she was smart, if she put her mind to it she'd been the smartest— But if she wanted to take off and go to a movie, say— Or the Poconos. She loved the Poconos. When she was old enough to drive—I remember one time, she wasn't even old enough—anyway, she'd drive us up to the Poconos. Just for the ride up and back. Sometimes we found a cheap place we'd stay over. I've *got* to call her." After reflecting, she went on with a smile. "We weren't the greatest workers, but once in a while we needed money we took odd jobs. We sold popcorn in a movie, but that was like two weeks—we weren't going to work every night, no way. Another job we had we worked for this caterer once in a while, waitressing, dishes. We— I'll tell you something interesting," she said then. "You know that man who was killed a few days ago? That Mr. Henning? We worked a party there last year."

For a few seconds Rick was too jolted to say anything. "What did you and Terri think of him?"

"He seemed very nice. Always smiled when you came up to him with a tray. It's a real pity. Terri, I don't know if she even saw him. Poor thing, she was stuck out in the kitchen."

Terri slammed down the receiver. Still busy. Her mother! Talk! Talk! Talk!

Denny said, "She ain't gonna report it."

"Who says? Tell me, who says?" This had to be the fiftieth time he said that, she didn't want to hear it anymore.

"I'm just sayin'," he said. "And who says she even *knows?*"

"She knows." And that must be five hundred times.

She had to think through all this. Even if she threw the .22 away, she was back to that thing she was always sure of: that somehow cops find everything. And, anyway, she wanted it, she wanted this gun, she wanted Denny to have his, only with a million more bullets. She wished she had a Uzi, too; a dozen Uzis.

She tried her mother again. Still busy.

She had to fight off the temptation just to pack up the car and beat it. Maybe go up to the Poconos. She couldn't think of the Poconos without thinking of that lake, without thinking of that house. Without thinking of Devore without the hate. But this time she was thinking of the house, of him, in a slightly different way.

She'd heard he had it up for sale a few years ago. She couldn't remember who told her, and she had simply accepted it. Not only that he'd put it up for sale, but that he sold it. If he had wanted to sell something, she had simply assumed he'd sold it.

She thought, then went over to the phone. She asked the operator for information up there, was told: 717-555-1212. She marked it down, then tapped out the number.

"Information."

"Do you have a number for a Mr. Walter Devore? It's somewhere near Hawley."

After a couple of moments: "I'm sorry, but that's an unpublished number."

"What's that mean?"

"The customer has asked that we not give it out."

She lowered the phone slowly, almost numb. Not only that he still owned it—it was that; but if the phone wasn't disconnected, it must mean they still went up there. Maybe on weekends, to ski.

She tried calling her mother again, but the line was still busy. Her eyes, though, had gone to Denny. He'd been putting some of his clothes in a backpack but had stopped and was looking in his wallet with a frown. He seemed to be counting the same bills over and over.

She said, "What's the matter? What did you spend?"

He looked startled. "Oh ... that damn bitch downstairs, this afternoon. Got me for eighty bucks."

"What d'you mean got you for eighty bucks?"

"Oh, I owed on last month's rent."

"You didn't tell me."

"Oh."

"What do you have left?"

"I don't know." He was obviously flustered.

"Christ, you've been counting it enough."

"Oh, it's twenty. Twenty-one. And I've got some change."

She looked at him as he went back to stuffing in his clothes. She had to stop herself being angry at him, for it wasn't his fault. "That's okay," she said, "we'll do fine."

She started to try her mother again, but instead her hand went to her handbag next to her and she opened her wallet and made a fast count. Five hundred and ninety-six dollars. Christ, the last she remembered she'd had a little more than seven hundred, and the thing was she couldn't remember buying anything that much during the past few days. Nothing! Well, a carton of cigarettes. Some newspapers. Yes, and there was that bottle of shampoo. And conditioner. Gas, they'd filled it once completely with gas, and once partway ... Screw it. Just then Denny, who she hadn't been aware was watching, said as she closed her handbag, "How much you got?"

"Plenty. More than enough. We're in good shape."

"Well, how much?"

"Over six. Plenty."

She went back to the phone, wanting only to get out of here, be on their way. And this time her mother said, "Hello?"

"Mother. Terri."

A gasp. "Terri. Oh, Ter. I'm so happy you called. You'll never know how hap—"

"I just want you to know I'm all right."

"I know you're all right, Terri. I'm so happy you called. You'll never ..." Her voice cracked; she couldn't talk for a moment.

"I just want you to know I'm all right," Terri said again, staring at Denny looking through drawers.

"Ter, we got such good news here. Dad's finally found a job, I'm working—"

"And I want you to know something else." She didn't want

to hear what her mother wanted to say. "I know you know, so I want to tell you. I want to tell you why. I had to get myself a gun. I have two friends were mugged. You can't walk out at night anymore."

"Ter, you'll be careful with it?" She didn't answer. "Ter, you've made me so happy. I was thinking all sorts of things, I'm ashamed to tell you how my mind—"

She stopped so abruptly that Terri, suddenly alarmed, said, "What were you going to say?"

"Nothing. I'm telling you, nothing."

"Mother, tell me."

"Oh, Ter. Don't be mad at me. I—I was so worried, it scared me so much, I had to ... tell someone. I told someone. But he's a good friend, he—"

"Who did you tell? What did you say?"

"Just that I ... knew you had a gun. I felt it."

"Who'd you tell?"

Her eyes were wide, staring at Denny. He was staring back, as though frozen in a position.

"A real nice person, Ter," her mother said. "You know that fellow I always read? I cut out his columns? Broder? Rick Broder? You know who I mean, Ter?"

*C*HAPTER TWENTY-SIX

He was driving on Banner Street, approaching Millway. If Mrs. McKenzie was right it was on Millway near this corner. He stopped at the intersection, looked in either direction through the street lighting but didn't see a florist's sign. He tried going to his right first, and several stores down he saw it, the sign lettered on the darkened window. There were two doors, one in the center of the store, the other apparently to the upstairs. And the upstairs windows were bright with light.

He had to circle the block since every parking spot was filled. When he came around he saw a space on the other side of the street, near the corner. Though some cars were in the way, by angling his head a little he could see the whole front door.

He didn't know what he hoped to see. Other than who walked in, who walked out. And if she lived here.

A blond, her girlfriend had said. A beautiful blond who from the time she was a kid had guys always hitting on her.

And now ... behind all this? A girl of nineteen? The .22 Killer who had part of the whole Delaware Valley—maybe half the country now, it seemed—had part of it cheering her on and another part looking over their shoulders in fear?

And that girl—he'd suddenly begun thinking of this; it

had gotten just a few lines in all of the stories—that girl who called Henning the day before he was killed?

Or was it all just coincidence? After all, the cops had a guy out there, maybe even had him now ... He was going to drop this in their laps soon, but not yet, not yet. *I trust you, I haven't even told my husband.* Mrs. McKenzie kept pushing her way into his mind. And maybe—he really couldn't get it straight—that was why he hadn't gone to them yet. That, but mostly the reporter still in him.

She said, desperation in her voice, and pushing the phone away, "The bastard, he's not listed!"

He said, "What about at the paper?"

"What about the paper?" she demanded. "What do we do at the paper? You know what he looks like? I don't even know what he looks like."

"Look," he said after a moment, trying to keep his voice down. "I mean, what does it mean? She told him you got a gun. She knows him. She told him. But everyone's got a gun. So? He don't know the make. Caliber. I mean, what does it mean? So you got a gun."

She'd thought of this, but it was as though once he knew she had a gun he knew everything.

"And like you say," Denny said. "Your old lady's a flake. If he knows her, he knows she's a flake."

Terri was trying to let all this sink in.

"I'm tellin' you," Denny said, "it don't mean nothin'."

She nodded soon, nodded quickly. She had a few more things to throw into her bag, and now, finished, they lifted the bags off the bed. They headed downstairs but then stopped at the foot of the steps, frozen by the same thought. Out there was the world. Out there was every cop waiting for them.

He said, "You wait here." Then he went out the back door, across the yard and out the gate to the driveway. He came around to Millway Street, stopped at the corner and looked over at the line of cars. All civilian, which meant nothing. He walked slowly, partway up the sidewalk. This one, no one; this one, no one; this one coming up, no. From where he was standing now he could see every car on this side of the street and they all looked empty. He looked over to the other side, without crossing. That one, no. That one, no. That— He stopped, suddenly.

He couldn't tell for sure from here, but there seemed to be a shape in the darkness in that one car. Whoever was in there, if there really was someone, couldn't see him back here, behind this car. Denny was tempted to go over and try to get a better look. But he was afraid he'd be seen. Instead he turned and, trying not to break into a run, walked back to the driveway. When they pulled out, he'd see if that car followed.

Suddenly Rick was sitting up straighter. The upstairs lights had just gone off. He kept his eyes fixed on the door. But several minutes passed and no one came out.

They—it was "they" in his mind; he pictured them together—they might not come out at all tonight, he realized. They could have gone to sleep, though it was only about nine-thirty. Or they could have just gone into a back room.

It was more than five minutes now. This was becoming stupid. It *was* stupid. But maybe not. He had waited almost a day, once, for a guy in a Burberry's coat to come out of a house, and following him, had opened up a scandal that brought down two judges. He had waited near a store for large chunks of three days, for the truck with cops out of uniform carrying out stuff. He had spent almost two months going through maddening statistics to—

But that was then, and this was now.

Driving here he'd searched the radio for news, that maybe they'd found that guy, that it was really all over. He was tempted to again, but in a perverse way didn't want to know. He kept staring at the door. And a minute or two later he saw two dark figures coming out and walking over to a car. He put his hand on the key in the ignition, waiting for just the right moment to turn it. He saw the headlights go on, then the car moving back and forth until it was able to maneuver out. He turned on the motor, but fought against pulling out and blazing the street with his own lights too quickly. But he couldn't let them get too far ahead. And almost in that moment another car went by, and he pulled out behind it.

He drove a little bit to one side so that they stayed partially in view. And then suddenly they were directly in front of him, the other car having passed them. He had to slow up, not to get too close. He wasn't sure, but he had the feeling it was a Mustang. And that there was a 3 and either a T or a P in the license.

They'd been going slowly for a while, but now speeded up. He stayed well back—too far back, it turned out, because another car pulled between them. But after about another mile that car passed them, too. He saw them heading onto the Expressway. West, toward the Turnpike, unless they cut off sooner. But no, the Turnpike.

Where the hell were they going?

He gave a little thought for the first time about turning back. But not seriously. He'd gone this far, and they were like a magnet drawing him on. They were two cars ahead of him at the ticket machine. Staying back a little he followed them east on the Turnpike, which would cross over into Jersey at the far end. But then about fifteen minutes later, seeing their right blinker light pulsing, he knew where they were going. This was the Northeast Extension, which led to a lot of places, but only to one in his mind. As her girlfriend said: the Poconos.

He glanced to see how much gas he had: half full. Not only was it too far to turn back now, he didn't want to turn back.

Though there were other cars on the road, it was easier to follow them now. He always let at least one car stay between them, but kept them in sight either by drifting out slightly or going on a different lane. But then about a half hour after they turned off onto 22, he lost them. He pulled onto the shoulder near a Dunkin' Donuts. He didn't know whether they had turned off back there somewhere or had just shot away.

There was nothing more he could do; he should just turn back. Let the police have it. Maybe Molly would be able to tell them if there was any special part of the Poconos she used to like to—

And then he saw what could be the same Mustang going by. He pulled out behind another car, then was able to draw close enough, and for just long enough, to see a 3 and a T. Then he drifted back again. But about forty minutes later he had a fast decision to make. They were pulling into a truck stop. He didn't know whether to follow them in or wait somewhere near the exit. He slowed up long enough for them to go in. He watched them pull up at the pumps, then he drove to where massive, darkened rigs were parked. He pulled between two solemnly-dark eighteen-wheelers. He couldn't see their car from here, but he could see the exit.

He had no idea what he'd do when they got to wherever they were going. It was as though he had come here without a thought.

Now and then he would glance at his watch.

Maybe it was the dark quiet, the dark silence of where he

was parked that made him start thinking of it. Of the cars that had passed their car, putting them in front of him again. Of their disappearing and then reappearing. As though they might have deliberately slowed up. And deliberately turned off in the hope he would too. And now, in here—

His motor was already on, and he quickly put the gear in Drive and was about to turn on the lights when just then he heard a loud tap on his window and he turned and saw a gun. It was held by a hand with a jacket over it, and the muzzle was against the glass, pointing right at his forehead. His first thought was to drop down or open the door, try to slam it against that hand. He started to open it, but the car, in gear, began to move. The gun cracked hard against the window, and both hands were on it now, following along with him. He stopped the car. The gun was directly at his face. One of the gunman's hands then made a little twisting motion toward the dash, and Rick turned off the motor. He took hold of the handle, started to open the door slowly, then swung it away and leaped out.

He felt the door hit something and he started to run to his left, but a car sat blocking the way. He cut toward an opening behind it, but knew he'd never make it first, then started to jump to the hood, to try to scramble or roll across it.

But the gun was against the back of his head now, under his ear. The pressure of the gun directed him to the door of the car, the Mustang. To where a girl was sitting behind the wheel.

The front door opened from the inside; the gun kept jabbing him into the back seat. The gunman slid in with him, shivering and holding the gun with two hands. All that Rick could make out of him was dark hair and T-shirt under an open sweater.

"Don't try no more shit," he said, out of breath. "No more, no more shit, no more."

She flung one look over her shoulder and now they were pulling away.

"Don't nothin'," the gunman warned. "Nothin'. You shit, you fuck, nothin'!" Then to her, "Turn on some fuckin' heat."

"It's on! It's been on!" There was a touch of hysteria in her voice.

"I'm freezin'!"

"You were out there, will you *wait?*"

"Don't move," he said to Rick, though Rick hadn't moved except to pull in breaths. "Don't the shit move!" Then, "You." He was still shivering, but in spasms now. "You, you him? You him? Tell me, you him? Her damn mother?"

"Christ, Jesus Christ," she screamed, with a fast look over her shoulder, "see he's got a gun!"

"Don't move," he said again. He was still breathing hard through his mouth. The gun closer to Rick's face, his left palm was hitting him around the chest now, then down around the hips. "Your wallet! Get it! And slow, goddamn you, slow, do it slow!"

Rick's hand came out with the wallet. Denny grabbed it, fingered it open, holding it up so he could see the license in its flap without taking his eyes off him.

"Him," but there was no surprise. He threw it to the front, to the passenger side. "Your crazy mother!"

Rick sat with his hands on his thighs. He kept looking at him, but then Denny cried, "Who the fuck you lookin' at? I'll smash your stupid face!" And even as Rick looked away, to look straight ahead, "I'll smash your face in, I'll shoot your face off! You hear me? You hear?"

Rick kept looking ahead. He knew that even one tremble of his hands, one quivering of his arms, might bring that gun, one of those fists, smashing against him.

"You okay?" Denny said to her. "You okay?"

"I'm okay. You be okay."

"I'm okay. Don't worry about me. Ho," almost singing it out, "don't worry about me."

He asked her to light a cigarette for him. She lit one for herself, too. Silence, a weird silence, them passing some cars, other cars passing them. She was holding it steady, controlled. "You okay?" Once in a while they still kept asking it of each other.

If I can grab his wrist or the gun.

But the guy wasn't even letting Rick face him; he'd have to whirl on him first, and that extra second would be a second too long.

Occasionally she'd glance back. Her eyes looked wild, but there was enough of a calm in her, apparently, that when Denny asked her to light another cigarette she didn't light one for herself.

"Nothin' now, you hear?" Denny to him, his first words in about a half hour. "Nothin'! You even blink! I swear!"

The road was mostly rural now, mostly climbing gently through hamlets, past farms, woodland.

"You got your lights on?" Denny said.

"Can't you see for Christ sake?" Her first real outward show of nerves in a long while. "What's the matter with you?"

"I meant are your brights on. You don't want your brights on."

"They ain't on."

Rick was hoping they'd start yelling at each other, that this guy would ignore him just long enough ... But they were driving silently now.

After about a mile Denny said, "Anywhere."

Just that, and the way he said it, and Rick knew. Tense,

trying to stay calm, he watched as she made several false turns off the road, always into woodland; always, she would slow up, stare through the hazy swath of their beams, then drive on.

Now. Try. Makes no difference.

But the gun, at the instant Denny had said "Anywhere," had gone pressed against his temple, stayed against it.

Rick's eyes followed the beams through several more aborted turns. His mind was racing, trying to grasp at something, anything. Now Terri completed a turn, a fast one, and they were driving along a one-lane road, woods on either side.

Something, anything!

The car was slowing up, then started to draw to the side.

Rick said, staring straight ahead, "The cops know who you are. I told them."

The car moved onto the rough shoulder, then stopped.

He said, "They were on their way. I was waiting for them."

Silence.

He could feel his breath quivering in and out. "When they catch up to you I'm your only chance of staying alive. Of getting away."

Still silence.

He didn't know if they were looking at each other. But the gun stayed pressed against his head. Then it jabbed against it even harder, as the car pulled away.

"Just stay this way, man," Denny said.

The gun was against his side now, though the only people around were over there in the office, not outside by the pumps or bays; they wouldn't be able to see it.

Terri had pumped the gas herself and was buying some things in the station's so-called mini-market. When she came out she was carrying two large bags, which she put next to her.

Then she tore open the wrapper of a little pie, ate it while driving with one hand. Denny was taking bites out of a candy bar, chewing hard.

An hour later they were heading down a narrow bumpy lane that looked as black ahead as it did here, but then as they came closer Rick saw shimmering under the vague moonlight that revealed it to be a lake. And, facing it, a house, completely dark.

Denny said, "Should I go up first? See?"

"Christ, no one's there. Can't you tell?" She swung the car up a small drive that led to a carport. She stopped, then drove around to the back of the house, then hesitantly on to the other side. "Good," she said, "good." Here the car would be walled in by large trees to the left and out of view from the lane.

She got out first, then Denny backed out slowly, motioning Rick on with his gun. A sharp wind was blowing in from the lake. Terri had a gun out now, was holding it to him with two hands, arms out stiff. He could make out Denny's outline moving about, but then he disappeared. When he came back he said, "Wait here. I'll bust a back window and open one of the doors."

The inside of the house was as black as outside and almost as cold. While Denny held the gun on him again, she was feeling her way around, stumbled against something but seemed to know her way. A light flickered on and off. "Ah," she said. "That was the refrigerator." So the electricity was on, though they didn't turn on any lights.

They took turns going to the bathroom, Rick last, Denny the whole time in the doorway. Then they tied his wrists behind him, then tied his feet together; pushed him down somewhere on the floor. They coiled rope around his chest, tying him to what felt like a square post. He couldn't slide down, had to sit.

He could hear them, at times, behind him. At other times they passed in front of him. He heard "there's food in the freezer." He heard that this meant "they used it, maybe on weekends." He heard her say, "This could mean they're coming up." Heard him say, "How do we know it'll be them?"

He could feel the house starting to warm up. Then out of the blackness a rag, a towel, something, went fast around his mouth, was tied in back. And he knew that his first job was to survive the night.

*C*HAPTER TWENTY-SEVEN

He tried to twist his fingers around to find the knot at his wrist. He squirmed and turned from side to side, straining to loosen the rope binding him to the post—but then after a last violent shaking, bent forward and fought for breath. He had to be calm, had to be smart. And the first thing he had to do, he knew, was control his rage, not only at them but himself. For being dumb. So incredibly stupid. It was only going to kill him, this rage: as much as the twisting and straining, it was tightening the ropes, tightening this thing going around his mouth that had his tongue coiled back to his throat. He had to breathe, try to control his breathing through widening nostrils. Just breathe. He tried not to think of this post against his back, this thing around his mouth, the pain in his wrists.

Just breathe. Go calm. Try to go calm. Think of calming things.

The creek—the creek he and Billy used to go to, with the woods where they were Tarzans, and the raft they built that floated though the water was around their ankles. His father, most everyone called him Doc; a quiet man, in a lab jacket; his mother in a lab jacket too, but no one ever called her Doc, though he didn't think until years later it was because she was a woman. Sailing, a million memories of sailing; he would again. Deirdre, her smile, the freckles on her face.

But it wasn't working, the rage was surging back. But only at them now. He would get loose, he would get out of this, and he would kill them. He would grab their guns, he would find a board, something, and smash them ...

And though this sent the blood rushing through him, it also enabled him to fall asleep, for a while.

Carefully she lifted Denny's arm from across her chest. He'd crashed out the second he hit the pillow, and she couldn't see how. She hadn't fallen asleep yet, it must be more than an hour now. He was breathing heavily.

She sat on the edge of the bed. It felt so queer, heart-hammering but queer, being back here. This was their room, the Devores; she and Robin slept in the next room, her brother in the room on the other side of the hall.

She'd felt her way in the darkness through almost all the rooms—everything was on this one floor, and everything seemed to her touch and from what she could see, pretty much the same.

She'd wanted to sleep in the other room, but Denny said no, come on, and that was okay, he was right. There were twin beds in there. But maybe what made this even more queer through all the excitement, was sleeping in this room. This is where he used to come back to after sitting on one of their beds telling them crazy stories. This is where he'd go in dressed one way and come out another. This is where if they ever screwed they screwed.

She got up and went out to the little hall where she could see into the living room.

She didn't know how Denny could sleep.

They not only tied him up, they'd placed chairs and some plates and other shit like that all around him so if he did get loose he would knock into something, they would hear. But even so. It was like he could do anything, especially at night. Like he had powers. Like the way he'd showed up. She could make out his figure now. It was lying still. She couldn't help it, but each time she'd come out to look at him she thought of him as ... it.

Back when she was a kid, there were these flapping, breaking sounds in the living room one night, and when they all came downstairs there was this giant dark bird on the floor, on its back, its long wings flapping weakly. It must have fallen in through the chimney. And her father had run out to the garage and come back with a shovel and broom, and carried the thing out, its wings still flapping between the broom and the shovel. And she'd rushed to one of the kitchen windows with her mother, and there he was smashing it with the shovel.

That dark figure over there was the bird. Only she couldn't kill it, not yet. And it was like tied to her.

It came to her, like a thunderclap, when she was back in bed trying again to sleep. What Denny had said back at his place, what he'd said then was still true! Nothing had changed! The only thing that made it seem like things had really changed was that son of a bitch being outside in his car.

But it was still true, all her mother knew was she had a gun. No caliber, no make, nothing. And that's all she could have told him. And when he called the police, *if* he called the police—where was her head? he could be bluffing—was, "Look, I hear this kid has a gun."

She took a deep, deep breath, then let it out.

Rick dozed off and on, finally waking after dawn, the

light filling the room. Again there was the struggle not to panic, just to breathe; to keep his tongue from coiling back toward his throat, to try to diminish, as though to a distance, the pain in his wrists, the burning around his ankles.

Gradually he took in the room, a living room, with maple furniture, mostly, and brightly-colored throw rugs. He could see, beyond the upended wooden chairs and dishes and pots that closed him in, the wooden deck in front and part of the lake. The pictures on the walls were mostly nature scenes, lakes and boats and mountains. There was a duck decoy lamp, and two true decoys, one on the mantel above the fireplace, the other on the TV. The post he was tied to was one of two that formed a kind of floor to ceiling entranceway to the back rooms.

The lamp table nearest to him, the one with the decoy lamp, had a couple of family photos on it. One showed a man and woman standing with two small children, a boy and a girl, in front of them. In the other, taken maybe ten years later, the boy was taller than his father, the girl was squeezing her mother's arm and grinning at the camera.

Were they the "they" coming here? All of them? Any two or three of them? Coming here to be slaughtered.

Not long afterward he heard a door closing somewhere behind him, then the flushing of a toilet. Later it flushed again. The two of them were out here now, she wearing a shirt that came just a little below her hips, her legs and feet bare. She was holding a gun. He was just in his jockeys, his arms folded over his chest, his right hand holding a gun, too.

They just stood there and looked at him. Then Denny bent down and touched one of the chairs, as if it might have been moved during the night.

Then they were behind him, in the kitchen; there was the sound of cabinets and drawers opening and closing, the clatter of utensils and dishes. Soon a kettle was whistling.

She came out to look at him, very briefly. But she went back in the kitchen only a minute or two more when she came out again, this time striding, as though she'd been suddenly enflamed. She pushed aside one of the chairs with her gun hand, kneeled next to him and pulled off the knotted rag. Denny was looking on.

"All right, tell me"—she was grimacing—"tell me what she said. My mother."

He just looked at her.

"All she told you was a gun! She told me! That's all! And this stuff you telling the cops! You didn't tell them nothin'. There was nothin' to tell."

He kept looking at her. If he said nothing she might kill him right here and now; if he said something she might kill him here and now. "I know about the party," he said, "at the Hennings."

Her eyes hadn't looked as if they could get any wider. "What about it? What do you know?"

Actually all he knew was that she'd worked in the kitchen. Molly out waitressing had barely spoken to her, and they had come and gone in separate cars.

"You tell me"—her gun was rising—"what do you know?"

"I know," he said.

"You know nothing, you know!"

He said nothing, kept looking at her in the eyes.

"You know nothing," but her voice was weakening. She stood up slowly. "You'll tell me okay," she threatened, but it was in that same voice. "You'll tell me all right, man."

She started to walk away, then stopped when he said, "I've got to go to the bathroom."

"Good."

But a few minutes later she and Denny were back. While

she held the gun, Denny gave more play to the rope around his feet, then untied one of his hands and brought both of them to the front where he tied them again. Then he opened the rope that held him to the post. After shuffling him to the bathroom he tied him to the post again.

The next Rick saw them they were both dressed but still barefoot, she in jeans and a tight red and white-striped sweater, he in jeans and a T-shirt.

He didn't know whether to say it, to give them the satisfaction, but he said it. "I'm hungry."

"You're hungry." She looked at him, then snapped a look at Denny. "Get him something."

"What do I give 'im?"

"What do I care? Anything."

Denny, smiling slightly, disappeared, then came back and tossed a Peanut Chew at him. Rick let it lay where it fell, on the floor by his hip. Denny stood there grinning now. When Rick, looking at him, still didn't reach for it he went over and turned on the TV and stood watching the screen as it came on.

"Keep it the hell down!" She was glaring at him from the sliding glass door to the deck. "Or turn it off!"

"I am, I am. I just want to see it works." It was so low he had to bend over to hear it. After a little while he turned it off, then looked over at Rick again. Denny sauntered off, then came back with a cup of coffee. He kneeled down but, smiling, held it so that Rick had to strain to reach it with his bound hands. The coffee was cold, almost gray. Taking little sips, Rick watched them. Wherever they went they took their guns, either holding them or setting them on something close by.

He heard her say, by the front glass, "I don't know, how can I guess? They'll come in either through the front or the side."

He heard him say, a little later, "I'm goin' out on the porch a while," and she, "The hell you are! You gotta stay in, don't anyone see you!"

Once, there was the distant sound of a car and, when he acted startled, she assured him it was from way back on the road. "You can tell," she said. "Christ, you can tell if it was comin' this way." She sounded so calm, she would even raise her cigarette to her lips so calmly, that it was almost more frightening, certainly more sinister, than her screaming.

And then suddenly the house seemed filled with the ringing of the phone. The two of them strode, as though trying to beat each other, to a nearby room. And from there, from an answering machine in what probably was a study, came a man's voice leaving a message: "Mr. Devore. Tony. Just want you to know I've got the cabinets and I'll be there Saturday morning. See you then."

Today was Wednesday.

*C*HAPTER TWENTY-EIGHT

She was grinning as she came back to the living room. She looked over at him, then at Denny, who was following her into the room. He didn't smile until he saw her grinning, and then it formed slowly and became a grin, too.

"That means," he said, "they'll be here either early Saturday or sometime Friday."

"Or maybe tomorrow," she said, "or even today. Who knows?"

"Today? You think maybe today?"

"Who knows? We won't know 'til we hear the car."

"I wonder how many of 'em," he said, almost to himself. "Maybe just him."

"Who cares how many?" she said.

His hips hurt him, his back, his neck and all the bones under him, from this hard floor, with just part of a throw rug curled under him.

He had to stop struggling against the ropes, he knew, even though the struggle was in his mind. It, and all this hate, was wearing him down.

Ever since they'd tied his hands in front of him, he'd

been trying to think of a way he could reach down and find the knot to the rope around his ankles, to the knot that kept him to the post. But not only were they out of reach, he couldn't even see them.

He'd even been thinking of a way he could reach one of the cups or plates they'd used to encircle him, somehow break one, use it to— But they took them away.

Once in a while one of them would come over and tug at the ropes. She would always stare at him, her face rigid. Denny would always stare at him too, but with a faint, twisted smile under those eyes.

Every few minutes, it seemed, they would go stand by one of the windows. Occasionally they would open the door to the deck or the one at the side and stand there listening.

"Over there," she said once, pointing somewhere at the lake, "is about where he freed that damn bird."

"Who?" he asked. "What bird?"

"You know, for Chris' sake! Him. And the bird, Christ I told you about the bird. You don't remember? We were all out fishin' and Robin threw out a line and a damn bird took it in the air and tried to fly away but couldn't, it was hooked. You remember? And her father brought it in but it dropped in the water, and he finally got it and got the hook out of its mouth and it flew away. I told you, for Christ sake."

"I don't remember. I'm sorry, I don't remember."

"I hate birds," she said.

Rick, watching, could almost feel her tension entering his. She would smoke, sit for a while, stand, go to one of the back rooms, come out again. Even when Denny didn't follow her, his eyes would. Once she called out to Denny from one of the back rooms, "All the same stuff, you know in all this time they still have most of the old stuff?" And Denny went in back to see, and Rick could hear him say, "These rich people, they hold onto all their old shit forever, that's why they're so rich." And twice within the same hour she picked up each of the pictures on the lamp table, looked at them, then set them down hard.

Through all of this, for most of the morning, she never said a word to Rick. But from the way she kept looking over at him, each time it seemed more intensely, he knew something was going to burst out.

It happened while Denny was in another room. She was sitting on the pine cocktail table in front of the sofa, the gun on the table while she was trying to put her bare feet into high heel shoes. She couldn't squeeze the second one on and she flung both of them across the room and then turned to him.

"You write junk, you know! A bunch of junk!"

He said nothing.

"'Ter-ri'"—a high voice, far beyond an imitation of her mother—"'listen to this. Ter, you know if you sleep on the top of your head ... Ter, you know if you keep hitting your grand-mother with a bat ...' Junk, it's all just junk!"

She was waiting for him to say something. When he didn't, she said, "You a doc-tor?"

"No."

"You went to coll-ich?" He didn't answer. "You went to coll-ege?"

"Yes."

Denny was in the room now, stood there smiling.

"That," she said, "why you think you know so much? All them books? All them per-fessers?"

He just looked at her.

Denny said, "Mister, all them books did, they got you into one hell of a mess."

"You're just shit," she said, standing. Her hand had hold of the gun now, by her side.

He told himself: don't say anything, everything will be wrong. But it came out anyway: "Why're you doing this?"

"You mean ... this?" Gesturing at him with the gun. And with a grin.

"What you're doing."

"You tell me! You think you know everything!" She came closer, raised the gun to his face, then bending toward him began screaming, "What do you know, what the hell do you know, goddamn you, what do you really know?"

Suddenly he was alone.

She'd left, whirling and standing up, with the same quickness she'd come at him. He could hear them in the kitchen now. For a couple of minutes all he could do again was try to control his breathing.

Soon he found himself looking over at the two pictures. It was hard at first to focus on the faces. All he knew for sure was that she knew them, had been here at one time. And that whoever they were, his life was tied up with theirs. And theirs, somehow, with Charles Wyndan's and Edwin Henning's. But how?

Wyndan, yes, her father had been laidoff. It was crazy, but still a motive. But what about Henning? She'd worked at one of his parties, but so what?

The only thing that seemed to link them was that each of them was rich. And since these two had never apparently stolen anything during the murders, it could be envy, jealousy. But he couldn't see it—not with these two kids—as something ideological that was having people calling talk shows and hiring security and spray painting billboards.

She was coming back to the living room now.

Denny said to her, repeating an earlier request, "How about it? Just a little? Just get out five, ten minutes?"

"Wait'll it's dark."

"Chris', I need to move around."

"Well, move around."

"Where? Walk around the walls?"

"They got one of them bikes back there."

"Where?"

"One of the rooms. Back there," she said angrily.

"But you gotta take it out."

"Jesus Christ, one of them bikes you exercise on."

"I didn't see it," he said.

"It's there. But if it makes a lot of noise, stop. A little noise. We gotta hear."

Soon Rick could hear the faint hum of the bike. She was standing by the glass door smoking, her back to him. He watched. Attractive—no beauty, though she could be—but attractive. And if not completely deranged, almost. He found himself wondering whose anger was greater, hers or Denny's. He had the feeling hers, not just because of the way she moved, looked, talked, but because she led in everything.

It made him think of *folie à deux*, where one person takes on another's craziness, though he didn't know if it even fit in here.

About a minute later she heard it, or at least reacted to it, a second or two before Rick. Barking. It came from somewhere in the woods behind the house. She strode away from the glass, went on one knee near Rick. Denny had heard it too, was kneeling right behind her. The barking would come close, then begin fading away, then come close again. It was as though the dog was running and barking all around the trees, maybe stopping to sniff.

Rick felt a gun against his temple. "Should," Denny whispered, "we close the drapes?"

"No."

They had left them exactly the way they found them.

"That little shit head," Denny said, strain in his voice, "is comin' closer."

It was, the barking was beginning to come down the lane.

Terri was holding her gun straight in front of her; the other gun remained against Rick's temple.

"Oh Christ," Denny whispered. Although the barking had stopped, they could hear paws coming up the steps to the deck.

And then from a distance, a man's voice: "Park-er! Park-er!" But the dog, a large golden setter, was at the front glass now, staring in at them. He barked a few times, then sniffed at the bottom of the glass, pawed it, trying to get in. He sniffed from one end to the other, then began barking again.

"I'm gonna let 'im in"—Denny was starting to stand up—"kill 'im."

Her gun went quickly to his chest. "Down, get down!"

"Christ!"

"Park-er! Park-er!" The calls were coming closer.

"If we let 'im in ..." Dennis pleaded.

"Shut up!"

The dog raised his head and howled.

"Parker!" The voice was at the side of the house.

And with that the dog whirled, scampered down the steps, and the barking went up the lane.

Denny sank to one knee, his gun arm across the other.

"You lose your goddamn head?" she said. Her face was flushed, but hard. He stood up and went to the side door and leaned against it, as if he might hear further sounds. "Christ," she yelled, "you put on the outside lights!" She ran to him, flipped down a switch on the wall. "You turned it on," she said savagely.

"I didn't know. It was an accident."

"Just hope he didn't see," she said. The two of them were facing the door.

"He couldn'ta seen, it's still light out."

"Just you hope he didn't see."

They were sure in about a half hour that he hadn't.

But it took a little longer for Rick to let go the hope of cars coming down the lane, or footsteps moving around the house.

CHAPTER TWENTY-NINE

Before dawn that Wednesday the first of the rigs parked overnight at the truck stop began pulling away, and by daybreak only a two-door black Saab stood in the area they left vacant. It stood like an invitation to come over, but if anyone driving in and out of the truck stop gave it any thought they didn't think it was anything all that strange: maybe it belonged to someone who parked farther away from the main building than he had to and was probably at breakfast or in the crapper.

It wasn't until after four when someone first wandered over, one of the mechanics. He walked around it, then tried the door on the driver's side and found that not only wasn't it locked but it wasn't firmly in place, that someone had apparently tried to shut it without full force. Still, he was hesitant about opening it, especially when, bending forward and shielding his eyes against the reflected glare from the glass, he saw a key in the ignition.

Going into the restaurant, he spoke to the manager who checked around but no one knew anything about the car or remembered ever seeing anyone in it or near it.

Within fifteen minutes a car from the state police barracks at Swiftwater pulled up. The trooper, in a Smokey hat and fur-collared, three-quarter length black coat, walked around the car, not wanting to touch it in the event it would be processed. From the windows he couldn't see any obvious signs of blood or a struggle on the tan interior, front or back. Just that puzzler of a key there, straight up, as if simply waiting to be turned and the motor to roar on.

The trooper walked to the back of the car to get the license number, and quickly saw something else as well. There was a sticker on the rear window that said PRESS. It was issued by the Philadelphia police and had an identifying number. A quick run-through of the license revealed that the car was owned by a Richard Broder, while a call from the barracks to Philadelphia led to the *Montgomery County Daily Dispatch* and, again, to Broder.

A woman who said she was the features editor told them in a deeply concerned voice that this wasn't like Rick, that they would be sending a reporter up there right away.

The officer said, "Would you please notify his wife or a relative and have them get in touch with us?"

"Yes. Of course."

Hanging up, she tried for several moments to give this a logical explanation, but just couldn't. As for relatives—and the word had such a frightening connotation to it now—she only knew of two; actually only one living anywhere around here. His mother lived in Florida—but she dreaded calling her and alarming her unnecessarily. But he had an uncle who was, or used to be, some kind of private eye.

Wally was with Sam when he got the call. He saw, with a feeling of alarm, the old man's face change; saw him set down his cigar to write things down as he asked fast questions, and then never once pick up the cigar again. Now, the receiver down, he sagged back in his chair and said, eyes wide and shaking his head, "Ricky. Missing."

"Jesus Christ. Where?"

"Poconos." Now he had hold of the phone again, was trying to tap out a number, did it wrong a couple of times in his hurry, and then finally reached someone he identified himself to. A cop up there, Wally knew now.

Mostly Sam listened. And then Wally heard him say, "And no blood," and Sam was nodding as though he couldn't hear this enough. Then he said, "I'm not sure, he's like thirty-six, thirty-seven, thirty-eight. I'm ashamed of myself, I'm not sure, I'm upset. He has like red hair, but not really red, more like brown ..."

Now, the phone down, he just stared at Wally, his face pale. It was several moments before he said, "Just his car. All they found was his car. At a truck stop."

"Anybody see him?"

Sam shook his head and held up his palms.

Wally, not wanting to press him anymore and not knowing what else to say, said, "You don't have a photo to give 'em?" although he'd heard him say on the phone that he didn't have one.

Sam shook his head again, said in a slightly bewildered voice, "The newspaper will be getting one to them," and then he leaned forward in the chair and called upstairs, "Esther?" She came down just far enough that he could look at her as he asked, "Do you remember the name of that young lady Ricky brought over?"

She tried, "Doris?"

"No," he said angrily. "Never mind."

Her first name began with a D, he knew that; knew her whole name in fact, her last name was somewhat similar to the name of an old Republican ward leader he used to know, but he just couldn't think of it right now. He wanted to reach her, maybe she'd heard something, knew something. Unless, and this added another layer of fear, that pretty little lady had gone with him and was missing, too.

But foremost in his mind was that woman, that Mrs. McKenzie. The last time he talked to Ricky, Monday, Ricky said she finally agreed to meet with him, told him she'd once called him at the radio station to talk about problems with her daughter, then had called him at the office to ask for help for her husband. And though she claimed that the police had cleared her husband, Ricky said he wasn't fully convinced she told him everything.

Wally watched as Sam stood up slowly from the desk. Then, as if just now thinking of something, Sam sat down again and after glancing through some papers, made another call. When he hung up without getting an answer, he said, "I was hoping Mrs. McKenzie ..."

Without a word he went to the closet for his coat and scarf and cap. Wally swung his own coat out of the closet and jammed his arms through the sleeves. At the door Sam called upstairs, "I'll be back."

They drove to O.L. Stein's. Went in. Mrs. McKenzie's back was to them as they approached her counter. There were no customers. When she turned, she smiled and asked how she could help them.

Sam said, "You'll excuse me, but I'm Rick Broder's uncle. You're Mrs. McKenzie?"

"Yes." The smile was still there.

"I don't like to bother you, especially here. But this could be very important. I know that my nephew, Rick Broder, talked with you. I'm wondering if you have any idea what might have taken him to the Poconos. The police found his car there, but he's missing."

She stared at him, and for an instant Sam thought the quick widening of her eyes, the slight opening of her mouth might be a normal reaction to such news. But he also detected what he was sure was a struggle for self-control. "I'm sorry," she said. "I've no idea why you think I might."

"I thought maybe something came up in the conversation. Maybe he told you something, maybe why he was going up there."

"No. I'm sorry. I'm very sorry."

"I see."

Sam had to force himself to walk away, wanted to grab her by the arms, shake her. But this had to be for the cops now. Fast. But he was afraid that they might take it as just an old eye's panic about someone he loved.

In the thickening darkness, Rick, contorting his hands behind him, kept trying to pick at the knot at his wrists. His shoulders ached as he twisted around, his fingertips were starting to burn. Each time they had to tie him again, like after the bathroom, seemed like a new chance; that maybe the knot wouldn't be as tight. But it still felt like a stone.

He didn't know if the two of them had left the room for the night or for just minutes; and after a pause for a few breaths he was digging at it again. And then he swiftly sat flat against the post. He heard a slight squeaking of the floor behind him, as though someone was just standing there. Perhaps watching. Then he saw a small, hazy light come closer and move about the floor, then shine on his face and his full body before moving away. It was Denny, bent over, his hand over a flashlight.

The light moved slowly across the floor, then showed the way as Terri came in. Now the two were sitting somewhere here in the dark.

Somehow he had to hold on to his sanity through another night. He didn't know how, when he couldn't even hold onto a full thought anymore, had only fragments of thoughts, bits and pieces. His car—would they somehow be able to trace it to him here? Deirdre. His uncle. And even those people in the pictures. He didn't want to think of them at all, but they came as though flashed on slides, the father lifting skiis onto the top of the car, the mother carrying a basket filled with—fruit? The daughter, the son. He even made up a son's wife, a daughter's husband. And all of them coming here.

"Ter!" It came almost like a hiss. "Listen!"

A radio—Denny's ear must have been pressed to it—went louder.

"... are still looking for Domen's attacker. The suspect, who police have not identified as yet, is said by police sources to have been laidoff by the Domen Tool Company. Police are also checking an unconfirmed report that he once applied for a position at Decker Barnes Pharmaceuticals. Now, turning to international news ..."

Denny snapped off the radio. Rick couldn't see their faces, couldn't tell what their expressions might be reflecting. But he wondered with a hot quickening through his chest if they were thinking what he was: if they leave here now, and kill me, they might be able to go home—and be in the clear.

Terri had to take a shower, even if it meant they could hear the water running a mile away. She bent her head into the water, let it flow down her hair that fell in front of her face, washed her hair with a new bar of soap she'd found in the closet, scrubbed it good, let the water run over it again, then pushed it back over her head again, squeezing it into a little ponytail. Then she luxuriated in the shower, holding her face up to it, her breasts, turning around, then lathered herself and went through it again, her face up, around, turning her back to the water. Then she reached in back for the handles and turned them off.

She sat on the edge of the bed in the towel, without drying herself. The jumpiness didn't begin again until then. And then it became more than jumpiness, it was what always happened; though she might look calm, she could barely hold herself in. And it wasn't just the Devores. It was the Devores, but not *just* them. He, that thing on the floor, represented everything she'd always hated. She even knew what he was like as a kid. He was one of those kids who always carried fifty books home from school, and wrote shit for the paper and were always making speeches in assembly and were on—what did they call it?—the de*bating* team. And when the kids became guys, they were guys who thought their shit didn't stink, and only went out with girls who thought their shit didn't stink either. Noses up in the air. Wouldn't even look at you. Phonies. Fairies. That's what she and all her friends called them.

"Ter?"

She hadn't been aware that Denny had come into the room; he was standing in the doorway, looking toward the living room. Then he came in, closing the door partway.

"Ter," he said softly, "how 'bout it?"

"About what?"

"What I started to say."

She had put what he'd started to say out of her mind. About beating it from here. Doing this guy, and beating it.

"Denny?" She stared at him in the dark. "You want to go? Go! I'll drop you off. I'll take you to a train. I'll take you to an airport. Just go! Leave me alone!"

"Ter, I didn't mean that."

"Go! I'm telling you."

"Gee, Ter."

"Then leave me alone! You hear me? Leave me alone!"

"I ... was just sayin', Ter."

She looked away from him, then stood up to dry herself. She didn't care if he went or stayed. And even if he stayed, she was going to do this one herself.

*C*HAPTER THIRTY

Rick heard footsteps in the dark, coming from the back, then saw her outline and the glowing tip of a cigarette moving toward the front glass. She was standing looking out there now, silhouetted by the hazy moonlight. He could make out the roundness of her hair, her hip-length shirt, her bare legs.

He pushed his tongue against the gag, to loosen it for a sound. He was so thirsty! Denny had made him reach for a can of soup, cold, but even that was back at about six. If he didn't get water— He let out a sound, but she didn't even turn. He did it again and tapped the floor with his feet.

She turned, the cigarette glowing in front of her. The smoke fanned out, the cigarette lowered, then went to her mouth again.

He kept making sounds, twisting his head from side to side.

He saw her silhouette bend forward, the glow of the cigarette arc down; heard a little gritty sound and she straightened up without the cigarette.

This time she came over, but stayed behind the barricade of chairs and whatever. He tried to say the word water, but it came out a hum. She kept looking at him. Then she pushed away a chair and, as though reaching to him from a distance, loosened the gag. It fell to his chin.

"Water. Glass of water. Please." She didn't move. "Please."

She kept looking at him, then left and came back with water. He bent his mouth to the glass, but after a few swallows he couldn't reach the water anymore and he tried to tilt the glass with his mouth. She lifted it up, but too fast, and the water spilled down his chin, but he kept swallowing. He began to choke, had to stop; then he motioned with his head again, almost forgetting he wasn't gagged, and she tilted it toward him again until he was finished.

Breathing hard, sucking air in through his mouth, he nodded at her. She kept watching him; curiously, it seemed. He nodded again; couldn't quite get his breath back—until he felt her trying to jam the gag into his mouth again. He twisted his head away, tried with all his strength to lift himself up against the ropes.

"Who are you," he gasped, "what are you?"

"This is what I am." Her hand went down to the floor, steadying herself as she kneeled, and now the gun was up against his cheek. "This is what I am! You want to know who I am?" He stared at her. "Who are *you*, huh?" she said. The gun pressed harder against him. "You're nothing! You're probably even a fairy! Nothing!" He kept staring at her. "A fairy," she said.

His eyes stayed on her. "You say," he said, very carefully, "I don't know anything. Why don't you tell me?"

"Shit," she said.

He wasn't sure, but he sensed that the gun was easing up just a little. "Why don't you?" he asked.

"Why"—he thought he detected a trace of a smile—"you want to write about me?"

"If you want." Still, very carefully. Just to keep her talking, whatever that would mean. "But that's not why."

"Oh shit. You don't know shit, mister."

"Then tell me." He paused, then, "Ter, why don't you tell

me?" He'd said her name deliberately, not knowing what would happen; and what it did was bring the gun harder into his face.

"Don't say my name! Who're you to say my name? Don't ever say my name again, you hear?"

"I'm sorry."

"Don't say my name."

"I'm sorry."

He could hear her breathing. "I know you," she said. "You got a wife and ten kids and you live out in Bryn *Maawr*. Right?"

"No."

"Villa-*no*-va? Glad-*wyne*?"

"No. None of that's right."

"You don't live on the Main *Line*?"

"I live in an apartment in Haverford."

"That's Main *Line*, ain't it?"

"I guess."

"And no wife and ten kids?" The gun kept prodding his cheek.

"None of it, no."

"You a *fairy*?"

"No."

"You're not married?"

"No. I was."

"And no kids?"

"No, we didn't have any."

"Why?"

"We just didn't."

She seemed to be thinking. "They'd have been bookworms, I bet." Then, "You always a bookworm?"

"I like to read. What about you?"

"Shit."

She was moving the gun slightly around one point on his cheek; it was almost as if she were feeling it with her finger.

He said, "Why've you been doing this?" She didn't answer. He said, "Your mother told me ... your father was laidoff, that ... he was angry, that he was threatening—"

"Him! All his life—all talk! Nothing but talk. Big man!"

"I thought ... maybe you did it because you were angry *for* him. Hurt for him."

"Look, you don't know nothin', mister! Nothin'! Look, I'm tired—" She reached over and tried again to get the gag back into his mouth, but again he twisted away. Or maybe, the thought struck him, she was letting him twist away.

"And Henning," he said, staring at her.

"What do you want, mister? That creep, that old— No old creep's gonna hit on me!"

"He hit on you?"

"Old creep!"

"And ... here. Why here?"

"What do you want, mister? What the hell do you want?"

Again the gun went harder against his face, but then it slowly withdrew. She was on both knees, staring at him; he could see her face clearly now. Then she turned her face away from him. It was a long moment before she looked back.

He wanted to say again, "Why here? Why these people?" but sensed it was pressing too close to whatever detonated her. Instead, though it was just as dangerous, though just about anything could be as dangerous, he said, "Why don't you give yourself up?"

She seemed startled. "You've got to be kiddin'."

"No, I'm not kidding at all. You know they're going to get you."

"Bullshit! Don't try giving me any bullshit!"

"It's not bullshit. It's just a matter of when. They—"

"Shut up!"—she was raising herself up to one knee—"*shut up!*" She kept staring at him, then grabbed hold of the rag and started working it back over his mouth, when all at once the light went on and she whirled. Denny was standing by the wall.

She screamed, "What're you doing?" and ran to him and turned it off.

"What're *you* doin'?"

"Get out of here! Get away!"

"I'm asking you, what're you doin'?"

"Get out! Get away!"

She strode back, loosened the knot to the gag, but only to tie it tighter.

CHAPTER THIRTY-ONE

It began snowing the next morning, Thursday.

"Den, look at this," she said at the glass.

He stood next to her, hands in his back pockets. "You think," he said, "it'll stick?"

"I hope," she said.

"Yeah, but maybe then they won't be able to come."

"Naah, they're skiers."

"Yeah, but what if it gets real deep? You know it can get awfully deep."

"I knew them, they had a four-wheel drive, probably still do," she said. "You own a place up here you gotta have a four-wheel drive. And they gotta meet that guy."

"It looks like it's gonna get awful heavy," he said.

"I don't know," and she slid open the door, letting in an icy rush of air. "No, it's real light ... I don't know."

"Maybe they'll come today, try to beat it," he said.

"I don't care when they come. As long as they come," she said.

Rick didn't know he kept dozing off, until each time he jolted awake, startled that he'd been able to give in to sleep even though he'd been awake every minute last night; even though his head, his eyes, were heavy with exhaustion.

But he had to stay awake. He didn't know what he could do, but he had to be awake. And he mustn't—a growing fear—hallucinate. He kept thinking he was hearing sounds, little sounds, tiny sounds. It panicked him because he thought it was in his head, a little tick-ticking; a water torture, only in some cavern between his temples. And then he saw what it was, saw it in the quick hits of snow on the front glass, the water trickling down.

He tried concentrating on his breathing but his mind wouldn't hold onto it. He thought for the first time about someone maybe having stolen his car before the police ever saw it—he hadn't given any real thought until now to the key in the ignition. Or even if the police did check it out, if they would get to his uncle. His uncle, he was sure, would lead them to Mrs. McKenzie, but he wondered if they'd have to follow the twisting route he'd had to take from there, to Molly, to learning about the Hennings—and then in some way to whoever's house this was, but probably no way before these people got here. And all this time the cops might still be looking the hell for someone else.

He looked at Denny, sitting on the arm of a chair, holding a small transistor radio near his ear. She was somewhere in the back. There was no reaching her, but maybe Denny might be the easier one; Denny who sounded like he was hoping for snow, for so much snow ...

She came back to the living room. A little later the two of them left, then only she came back. Soon after that he joined her again.

"You think it's stoppin'?" he said. "Looks like it's stoppin'."

She stuck her hand out the door. "I don't know. A little."

"I think it's goin' to be tomorrow," he said.

"I don't know. We'll see."

For the first time he was aware that they'd opened the side door a crack, so they could hear a car better. They had something holding it, so it wouldn't blow all the way open, and now and then one of them would go back to check on it.

Once when she went in back she was gone so long that Rick started to say something, but almost at that instant he could hear her coming back.

But now, when she left, he heard a door close on the other side of the house. Either one of the bathrooms or a bedroom. Chances were, the bathroom.

Denny had turned off the radio and put it on one of the lamp tables. For the past couple of minutes he was standing looking out the front.

"You're not even making any money out of it," Rick said. Denny turned slowly. "Not even any money."

"You"—Denny was pointing—"shut your mouth."

"Tell me. You're going to kill me anyway. I don't understand something. What's in it for you?"

"Listen, you." He came closer.

"It's not even you're the town hero anymore. Go twenty-two. I could understand that. But it's gonna come out, all you did was hurt people. And am I right, it's her people, not even yours."

Denny swept up his gun from a table.

"Denny, listen. You don't have one chance, not one. Look, they've had to have found my car by now and they'll know I've been talking to her mother and I was out looking for Terri. And they'll find out about this place ... Denny, all you're going to do is get killed, get both of you killed."

"I'm warnin' you ..." But the gun hung by his side.

"You give yourself up they'll know you could have hurt other people. They'll know. And I promise you I'll do whatever I can to help."

Denny kept staring at him. For a moment he looked perplexed, agonized. Then his eyes widened and he whipped the gun up and strode forward, fast.

"Go fuck yourself! Fuck you!" And now he was yanking Rick's head back, was gagging him again. Then he grabbed hold of a length of overhanging rope at his legs and tied his legs back to his arms.

"What's amatter?" She'd raced in from the bathroom.

"He was sayin' there's nothin' in it for me! No money, your people! And they're gonna get us! They got his car, they know he's been lookin' for you, they'll learn about here!"

"You *listenin'* to him?" she screamed. "You listenin' to *him*? They know nothin'! That car's a million miles from here, and I ain't been here in years, and all I ever did anyway was drive around. You listenin' to *him*?"

Denny stared from her to him. Then, "Fuck you!" into Rick's face. "You hear me? Fuck you! You're dead!"

"Keep it down," she said.

Wally said, "Why don't you call? Why don't you find out?"

"I will," Sam said. "I want to give 'em more time."

They'd gone to the police about five yesterday; it wasn't quite noon now. Sam had been sitting by that phone ever since Wally got here this morning.

After a few minutes Sam said, "You don't think it's too soon?"

"No, and so what? If it's too soon it's too soon." Wally hurt for him—the Boss wasn't timid, it had to be he was afraid of bad news.

Sam's hand went to the phone. He spoke now to the cop they'd gone to, an old friend of Sam's who used to work for Wally. He was to have passed their suspicion along to the chief cops on the case.

Hanging up, Sam said, "He'll get back to me. He don't know, he just got in."

Ten minutes later the phone rang. Sam had it before the first ring ended. Less than a minute later he was holding the receiver down on the hook. "Mrs. MacKenzie," he said, "told them she had no idea why Rick went up there."

*C*HAPTER THIRTY-TWO

Early that afternoon in response to his muffled sounds, she lowered his gag.

"Do me something," he said. "My legs are all cramped. Untie them. I'm not going anywhere, my feet are tied."

She looked at him, then slowly untied the rope that bound his legs up behind him. She tossed it to the side. He nodded thanks. His thighs, his calves felt on fire. After several long breaths he said, "And I'm hungry."

He was surprised to see her come back with a glass of milk, the first sane nourishment they'd given him. As he tilted his head back to drink from her hands, his mind was racing to how he might get hold of the glass, hide it under him, break it at night, use it— But it was, he was aware, another of the escape plots he kept coming up with that took his full energies until he realized they were crazy. Like the one he'd had about stumbling against the light switch on his way to the bathroom and turning on the outside lights, even though someone would have to be staring directly at them to see them in daylight, and at night they would illuminate the windows. And all the other schemes about somehow grabbing one of their guns ...

Finished, he said, "Wait," as she started to work back the

gag, and he strained to wipe his wet stubble along each shoulder. "Thanks," and then, to talk and maybe get her to talk, he said, "Tell me, what d'you got against bookworms?"

She rose up slowly. "Shit," she said sullenly. Then to Denny, though with a little smile, "Shit."

"Christ," Denny said. His back was to the front glass.

He came over to put back the gag, and Rick said, "Give me a couple minutes, will you? You got a gun, I'm not going to yell."

"Leave the sucker," Terri said.

Denny went back to the glass and turned and watched him.

After a few moments Terri said from the kitchen, "Bookworm. Tell me. Did you used to go to proms?"

"Some."

"You take a limo-zeen?"

"No."

"What kind of rich kid were you?"

"Who said I was rich?"

"Did you go out with snooty girls?" She was still back in the kitchen.

"I don't think so, if they went out with me."

"Ain't you funny," she said.

"Hey, what's this shit?" Denny said, coming forward. "I don't want to listen to this shit."

"Oh, let him. I'm havin' fun."

"I don't want to listen to this shit," Denny said. And he put back the gag.

Twisting, squirming, Rick tried to reach the knot at his wrists behind him. One fingernail touched a crack in it, tried to pry it apart, but he had to stop, his whole hand ached.

He leaned back against the post. But just for a few moments. They'd be back here any second—he could hear them moving around in the back rooms—and now his hands were curving and twisting to reach that tiny crack again. He had it again now, but as he struggled with it he felt a little pain in the nail of his right index finger, was sure he'd torn it.

He leaned back again, then his fingers went back to the knot. He couldn't use his right index finger anymore, strained with the left. He could feel the crack now, tried working the tip of his finger into it. Was it spreading? He twisted his wrists from side to side, but that might only be tightening it, and he dug the tip of his left index finger into the slight opening, was working it.

And then quickly stopped.

Terri had come back in the room, was standing looking out the glass. Soon she turned and looked at him. His eyes stayed on her eyes. Then she strode over, hesitated a moment and pulled down the gag.

"How she come to tell you?" she said. "My mother. About the gun."

"She was worried about you. She was worried about you before she even knew you had it, and then that scared her."

"Lame brain. All your junk she has. Lame brain."

"Why's she a lame brain?"

"Oh shit. Takes shit. Lives with that guy."

She turned to look out the window again. He looked at her. He was sure she wanted to talk more, or she wouldn't have left off the gag. But at the same time, he couldn't forget that anything he said could set off an explosion.

He said, "Can I ask you something? About this place?"

She whirled. "What about this place?"

"Did you used to come up here a lot?"

Glaring: "How do you know I came up here at all? How do you know that?"

"I heard you saying. About fishing with someone named Robin and hooking a bird and her father freed it."

"Oh, that."

After a moment, while she was looking out the glass again, he said, "Who are they?"

She whirled again. "Shut up! Will you shut the hell up? Shut up!" She started to look away, then stopped and said, "Robin—that goody-goody little girl. And her *Daddy*! And that family—it used to get me sick, I never saw people kiss so much. And *him*, what a phony, what a rich phony. 'You're'"—and her voice went low in imitation—"'you're such a good friend for my Robin. You're so funny and you're so smart.' Christ. And I believed he meant it. Then they send her to another school, they even move from the whole neighborhood. Like I was a bad in-flu-ence. Like because of me she started making out. Like she never made out before!"

He watched as she took a couple of deep breaths. He said, "Were your parents friends of theirs?"

She grinned. "Yeah, sure, him and my father in particular, they were real tight. Shit. I don't think he'd have even let him wash his Mer-say-dees. My father!" she said fiercely. "Big shot. Like he ever did anything. And yet yellin' at me I'm a bum, I don't have any brains. 'Who thinks like you? I don't know anyone thinks like you. You'll never be anyone, you'll always be a bum.' Christ."

Rick waited before saying, "Can I ask you something about your father? Did he abuse you, your mother, the—"

"What're all these questions?" she suddenly demanded. "What're all the questions?" But then, almost instantly, "I'd have put a knife through him he touched me. Or touched my mother. But he's all mouth, all mouth. Like, Christ, they fire 'im and he's yellin' all the things he's gonna do to 'em, but he still walks around wearin' their T-shirt. Wimp!"

He wanted to say, "And you showed him, right?" but he saw that Terri was looking away, was looking over at Denny who had materialized at the opposite side of the room.

"I want to talk to you," Denny said to her.

She stared at him, as though angered by his presence, then slowly followed him. She watched as Denny closed the bedroom door behind them. They stood facing each other.

His face was fiery. "What's goin' on?" he demanded, his voice quivering. "What're you always talkin' to this guy for all the time? Your mother! Your father! What d'you keep talkin' to him for? If I didn't come out you'd still be talkin' to him!"

"Denny, leave me alone."

"I kept tellin' you don't talk to him. I *asked* you! How many times I *asked*? But no, you gotta talk to him. 'Tell me,'" his voice in a high falsetto, "'about your prom. What kind of girls did you take? Did you take a limo-zeen? My mother saves all your ...' I asked you! I said don't talk to him!"

"Denny, cut this shit."

"What the hell is it? You like him? That why we haven't done him? You like him? The bookworm? I thought you hated bookworms! You want 'im to read to you? Your mother's got a thing for him, you got it, too? You got a thing for him, too? You wanna sit on his lap and—"

She began flailing at him, wanted to smash that ugly face. He ducked away, holding his arms out.

"You know I kept askin' you."

"Get outta here! I'll kill you! I swear! Get outta here! I don't want to see you. I'll kill you, I swear!"

He stared at her, breathing through his mouth. Then his body seemed to go limp. He slumped down on the side of the bed, stared at the near wall.

"We're through, you hear?" she shouted. "Through. I'll kill you I have to look at you."

"Oh geez, babe." He put a hand to his forehead.

"Kill you." Her chest kept heaving.

He began shaking his head slowly, to himself. "I'm sorry, babe." But it was almost a minute before he could look at her. "I don't know— I'm jealous. I'm scared. I'm sorry"—he looked close to tears—"you believe me?"

Gradually as she stood looking at him that face was losing its ugliness, was becoming ... just Denny again. She sat down next to him. She let him take one of her hands.

"You believe me I'm sorry? I didn't know what I was sayin'."

"What'd you have to say about my mother? That shit."

"Will you believe me I didn't know what I was sayin'?"

She wasn't completely down from it yet, but she said, "If you say."

He tried a half-smile. "Did you mean it you said you'd kill me?"

"Sure." She said it with a smile, like that made it silly, but though it was becoming hard to believe now she had meant it.

"Ter?"

"What, Den?"

"Let's swear something. Let's never fight again. Let's swear to it."

"We're never going to fight again," she said, looking at him.

He put both arms around her; his head went against her shoulder. "I'll never do that again. I swear."

She held onto him. After a few moments she said, "Hey," lifting his face, "you're shaking."

"No, I ain't."

"Den," she scolded lightly, "everything's gonna be okay."

"You mean it?"

"I'm *tellin'* you."

"You're not worried?"

"No, I'm not worried," she said, imitating him.

"Then why— You don't know I see it maybe, but why do I see you countin' our money all the time?"

"I don't do it *all* the time. Christ, I want to see what we got."

"How long you think it can keep us goin'?"

"Den. They're coming up. They're gonna have money. And if I know them, they're gonna have all kinds of credit cards. And hey," she added with a grin, "worse comes to worst we're gonna have to rob a bank or two."

"Yeah?" He smiled. "I never robbed a bank. I never robbed nothin'."

She felt the sudden need to keep talking. It was as though once she stopped, even paused, she would be all alone with the beating of her heart.

"Tell me," she said, "where you'd like to go."

"You mean anywhere?"

"Sure. Anywhere."

"I don't know," he said slowly. "I never been nowhere much."

"How about Paris? Would you like to go to Par-is, France?"

"Yeah. I'd like that. Would you like that?"

"You kidding? Or Mexico. Anywhere."

"Jesus."

"Den, you're still shaking."

"Nah. It's ... just that it got cold in here. Ain't you cold? I don't know what happened to the damn heat."

If anything, she was too warm. "Let me." She brought him to her and began rubbing his back.

"That feels so good," he said softly.

Soon she felt him lift up and touch her cheek. He was turning her face to him so he could kiss her mouth. She really didn't want this now, she just wanted to hold onto him, but she let him.

"Ter," he said, his head against her breast, "do you like me?"

It startled her. For a few moments she thought it was a stupid thing to ask, but then she couldn't remember ever saying it to him. Or certainly ever telling him or *anyone* she loved him. "Are you kidding?" she said. "You kidding?"

Rick almost let out a little gasp.

He felt one piece of the rope moving. His left forefinger hooked under it, had it yielding. But almost immediately he had to stop, to ease a cramp—his whole arm ached. Now he was back at it again, had that one piece falling away, was reaching for the coiled segment behind it. He began twisting his hands, not knowing whether he was tightening or loosening it more, then stopped again, thinking he heard a noise behind him.

But nothing.

About half an hour ago he'd heard them shouting at each other in one of the rooms, but there'd been silence after that.

Now, after a quick look behind him, he was digging at the knot again. It *was* a little looser, just a little. His left hand ached so much that he had to use his right, but that had the torn nail on the index finger. He used his middle finger, exploring, scratching. He thought—then was sure—that here was another opening; he could feel it. He lifted at it with that finger, lifted, poked, pulled, and after a few moments it gave, and he squirmed that finger into the hole and widened it. The rope loosened beneath the flurry of his fingertips.

Only to expose another knot underneath.

He fell back. He tried yanking his wrists apart, then squirmed around until his wrists were against a corner of the post. He kept rubbing the knot against it, rubbing hard, harder, hoping that some part of the rope would catch hold, give just a fraction, and then he slumped back, exhausted. But soon his fingers were twisted around again, reaching, feeling. And he thought he felt, but he wasn't sure, a slight loosening.

A few minutes later he heard them coming out, and he squirmed back to sit facing squarely ahead.

"We should have bought beers," he heard Denny say.

"We'll get plenty of beer soon," she said.

"Yeah?"

"Sure. We'll get it."

They both came out smoking cigarettes. Denny glanced over at him but she didn't.

"Look at it out there," she said.

Night was against the glass, and there was a dark border of snow along the bottom. She went over to the door. "Hey, look at this," she said. She'd slid it open and was standing looking out at the snow.

Denny came over and stood with his hands on his hips.

"That's *deep*," he said. Then, "Where you goin'? You're barefoot."

"Come on."

Rick watched them walk out onto the deck. When they came back in she had a mound of snow between two hands.

"Here," she laughed, and flung it at Denny's face.

"You rat! You dog!" He went out and came back with snow and flung it at her, then ran out again and flung some more. She was scooping it off her hair, her shoulders, and throwing it back at him. Then she hurried out and brought back more, and he ducked behind a chair, and she raised her arm—only to bring it down slowly, her eyes wide.

She'd heard the sound of a car coming down the lane. And its beams were now gliding along the side windows.

She closed the glass door, he the side door. She was behind a chair, facing the front, he next to Rick, angled toward the side door, his gun leveled over Rick's head. Rick, his legs tied in back again, pressed his head back against the post.

There was silence now, as the motor died. Then there were voices, clear in the night: a man's, a woman's, maybe one or two others.

"We'll get those later," the man's voice said.

"What about the bags?" a woman asked.

"Let me get that one," he said.

Car doors opened and closed.

"I'll turn on the outside lights," he said.

"Watch yourself. The steps. Let me help."

"Robin," he said, laughing, "help your mother, she's gonna break her beautiful neck."

There were footsteps coming up the stairs now, to the deck.

Rick watched the front. He had only a vague idea, it hadn't really come to him until now, didn't know if it would work, knew only he was dead, that— He heard the key turn in the front door. It started to slide open. And he immediately lifted himself on his right hip, then bucked and let his feet hit the floor; started to lift them again when there was a smash against his forehead.

Dazed, almost out, he heard gunfire, screams outside, the sound of a car screeching away; then a voice, Terri's, screaming "No don't, we still need him!" and now someone was dragging him out, stumbling, into the snow.

*C*HAPTER THIRTY-THREE

Snow was hitting his face; it was deep to around his ankles. They'd cut his feet free, but it was hard maneuvering down the steps, with Denny pulling him. One of them shoved him into the back of the car, and Terri, still working an arm into her jacket, followed him in. Denny, clutching his jacket, was trying to clear the snow from the windshield with his bare arm, then bent his way in behind the wheel, closing the door with his gun hand, trying to start the motor with the other. It kept whining, he kept pumping away at the gas. "You'll flood it, goddamn it!" she yelled, and he yelled back, "You try, you—" But now it was going. The windshield wipers, faltering at first, moved slowly against the collecting snow.

Rick's head, pulsing, kept sagging toward his left shoulder, toward her. He wished he could just lift his hands to it but they were still tied in back. He could feel, as though distantly, her gun under his ear.

"You bastard, you bastard!" Denny began yelling back at him. And to her, "Why didn't you let me kill him? Why? *Why?*"

"Shut up!" she screamed. "For Christ sake, you'll get us killed, get outta here!"

"Shoulda let me—" But he was fighting a long skid now,

still on the lane. He turned onto another lane, then another. "Where'm I goin'? I don't even know where I'm goin'."

"Just go!"

"The fuckin' windshield wipers!" The wipers were faltering again, against little clumps of ice.

"Just go!"

"They see you?"

"How could they see me, there was no lights! For Christ sake!"

"You hit him? You hit anyone?"

"I don't know. No. Just go."

"They couldn't have seen the car. So they got nothin'."

"Just go."

"Oh, you bastard," he said to Rick. "You wait. You just wait." A little later, he said, "Oh Christ." The wipers had stopped. He tried driving on but the snow kept piling up. He opened his window and reached around but couldn't get to them. He pulled over to the side and jumped out and had them going again. "Christ, we need heat," he said. He still had only one arm in his jacket.

"Then turn it on, for Christ sake!" She leaned forward a little, as though to help him reach it. Rick could feel the gun slipping around under his ear, and an instant's thought was that if only his hands were tied in front he could swing at her.

"Where we goin'?" Denny was saying. "I don't know where I am."

"Just drive."

"I don't know where I am!" Hysteria edged his voice.

"Will you just drive? No, lemme drive."

He whirled. "Whyn't you let me kill him? Fucked us! Whyn't you?"

"You moron, I told you. The cops! They'll be bringin' the

cops! This place will be stinkin'. We still need him. When we don't need him—"

"I said don't talk to 'im!" He was back to that, screaming. "Talkin' to him all the time! Just like your mother. Whyn't you let me do him? I was right, you like 'im. Just like your mother! All 'ese freakin' bookworms you said you thought shit!"

"Stop this car!"

But he kept driving. "He jinxed us! Fixed us!"

"Stop this fucking car!" She was leaning toward him. "Stop it! Pull over!"

"I'm drivin'." But his voice had lowered. "Just sit back."

"Look," she screamed, "you wanna kill him? I've had enough of this shit! I told you why. Now if you wanna kill him, kill him. Stop the car. Go ahead stop, pull over, kill him!"

"Come on, Ter, I—I'm sorry ... I'm just lost."

"Or I'll kill 'im! I'll kill him right this second, right here, right now. Pull over! Or I'll do it you're drivin'."

"Ter, where are we?"

She settled back. It was a minute or two before she was able to say, "How the hell do I know, I don't know."

Then a few minutes later he cried, "Oh Christ."

Ahead, the sky over a hill in the road was sparkling with police lights, coming closer. Denny, after a moment's hesitation, raced ahead, as though to crash through or speed by whatever was coming up that hill, then he saw a narrow opening in the woods to his right and bumped and jolted through, crashing bushes. He killed the lights and motor, and soon afterward the lights went by behind them.

They stayed there about a half hour. The only thing Denny said was, "I'm sorry, babe." And the only thing she said was, "We'll do 'im. We'll know when."

***

They backed out slowly, after Denny rubbed the windows clear with his sleeve. But the snow was already starting to pile along the arc of the wipers and against the rear and side windows.

She said, "We gotta get outta here. Far."

"How do I get out," he said frantically, "when I don't know where we are?"

"Just go. Go."

Ten minutes later he said, with the same desperation, "I still don't know where we are. I wish to hell I knew." It was as black here as it had been back around the house. They must have driven about ten miles, though part of it could have been circling back and forth. There were snowy trees and fields on either side, and only an occasional light among the scattering of houses, most of them at a distance.

After about another mile he said, "Oh Christ." The wipers were doing it again, stopping every few seconds before leaping forward and then stopping again. And now both wipers were stopped halfway in their arc.

And this time, though he got out and pulled at them, he couldn't get them started.

He tried to drive some more, reaching out and making a clear spot with his hand, but he had to keep doing it every minute or so.

"What'll we do? You bastard," whirling on Rick, "oh you bastard!"

"Just park," she said. "Keep the heat on."

"We ain't got all that much gas."

"Well, just keep goin'. Let's see maybe a house."

The first one they passed was dark, but there was a car in front. The second one was dark too and had no car, but it was too close to the road. And the third, though she was tempted, was just as close. Then she saw the dark shape of a bungalow, set back a little among the trees.

They drove up to it slowly. There was no car that they could see, and when Denny got out and looked he saw there was no garage. When he came back, she said, "Just go up. Ring the bell."

He went up to the front door, his gun behind him. After about five minutes he came back. Nothing. She said, "Pull around the back."

But the snow was even thicker back there, and the wheels started to spin. Denny turned off the motor and got out, with Rick maneuvering out behind him and Terri right in back, holding a gun to his head. There was the sound of breaking glass, and now they were entering the dark house, where her first words were, "It's freezin'."

But Rick was aware only of the slight crackle of glass under his feet. He pretended to stumble, went to one knee, then on his back. But Denny, cursing that he'd almost tripped him, yanked him up before he could even touch a shard of glass.

CHAPTER THIRTY-FOUR

Denny pulled him along through the blackness, then pushed him to the floor of what seemed to be a front room, either a living room or a den, and tied his feet together.

"Christ, I'm freezin'," Terri said, her voice shaking. "I'm freezin'."

The only things she'd been able to grab up in the scramble were her jacket and her handbag with the money and bullets but her feet were bare and the legs of her jeans were wet to her knees. She was hugging herself tightly, trying to control the shivering. The gun in her right hand was shaking near her cheek.

"Lemme see," Denny said, his voice quivering too, "if I can find a thermostat."

She saw the vague outline of him move off, to feel along the walls. She heard him bump into things, curse, then there came a burst of little rattling sounds, which he called out were empty hangers in a closet he'd opened.

"What're you openin' closets for?"

"I made a mistake! I felt a knob. Christ, I can hardly see."

She looked down at the dark figure at her feet. She had to fight against bending over with this gun, bending over real close, and just emptying it into every part of him. Because of him, because of this scum bag, Devore got away. And if it wasn't for him no one would have even known who they were in the first place. Why hadn't she let Denny kill him? Or, better even, killed him herself?

"Found it," Denny called.

When he came back she said, "One of us gotta watch the front, the other the back."

"Ter, no one's stayin' here, no one's comin' home tonight. These gotta be summer people. That empty closet—"

"Just listen to me," she said sternly. "Okay?"

"Sure."

She didn't want to scare him more than he was, but what an asshole. Didn't he know that an alarm must have gone out for miles around? And that these cops knew which were summer homes, which shouldn't have a car outside?

She wanted to go out and try to move it deep among the trees. But she knew the car must be snowed in. And her feet were like blocks of ice.

She groped her way toward the back. Her eyes were becoming used to the blackness, could make out shapes and even things. She opened a closet but it was empty, then another, and this one had towels and thin blankets on the shelves. She grabbed a thick mass of them.

The rear bedroom, she found, had a window facing the driveway, and a second window the trees in back. Heat was coming from a register in the far wall. She took off her jeans and put them on a chair in front of it, then stood almost against the register for a while, blankets gathered around her. Then she went to the side window and dragged over what felt like a small love seat.

But though she was warmer, she couldn't stop the shakes.

So close ... that goddamn Devore, that *hypocrite*, had been so close! And that daughter of his who was going to coll-ich! And Miss-us Devore, who was no better. And whoever was with them!

Oh, she couldn't wait, she couldn't wait to do that ugly thing in the front room.

Maybe tomorrow, if they could get out of here.

But whenever. One thing she was still sure of was that somehow they would be getting away.

She woke up startled that she'd fallen asleep in the chair.

For an instant she felt a kind of pleasant glow. She didn't know whether she dreamed this or had been thinking of it before she fell asleep, but she remembered it being morning and they'd been able to shovel out the car.

Now her heart was pounding, as if all this was new.

It was still black out there.

Grabbing up her gun, which she'd placed on the window-sill, she made her way to the front room. She could make out Denny sitting on a chair by a window; that thing, its head turned toward her, on the floor.

"You all right, babe?" Denny said.

"I just wanted to see," she said, "you didn't fall asleep."

Rick felt for an instant she'd caught him, partly turned to one side and his fingers working back there. He waited until he felt sure she was gone, then began picking at a loop he'd enlarged. Denny was about fifteen feet away. Most of the time he was staring out, but every so often he would look this way or go to one of the windows at the side.

Heart racing, Rick tried separating his wrists, and they came apart a short way before the rope tightened. That was better, a lot better, but far from there.

He was lying flat on the stone floor, away from the throw rugs, without anything to sit up against. He could only reach the knot by going slightly to one side or the other.

Once, seeing him shifting position, Denny taunted him with, "Want a mattress?"

"My hips hurt."

"Yeah? Just think of the long time when they won't hurt anymore."

Right now he had another loop in the knot. His fingers began scrambling around, trying to pry open whatever they touched. Then he lay back, out of breath. What would he do even if he got free? His fingers were almost raw, and he'd ripped the torn nail even more. He curved and twisted them again, scratching at the rope, pulling, and now began yanking his wrists from side to side. The rope began giving a little, slowly. It gave almost a foot before locking. He didn't know if it was because the rope was so entwined back there, or whether it would take just an extra pull for it to come completely apart.

He said, "Can I sit up? The floor's killing my back."

Denny said nothing, though he looked over. The silence was part of the taunting.

"Can I?"

When he still didn't answer, Rick struggled up anyway, with Denny watching. It seemed like almost a minute before he looked away.

Rick could feel the rope drooping in back of him. He tried, by degrees, separating his arms even more. They widened. Though rope lay curled over both wrists, it felt ready to unravel. He stared at his legs. No way could he untie them without being seen. And Denny was too far to reach, hopping.

He stared around through the darkness. A fireplace made up the nearest wall, a stone fireplace, but he saw it only in passing. He was looking for something he could use as a ham-mer—a small lamp, a heavy ashtray, anything. He thought of calling him over and trying to strangle him with the rope. Then he made out what looked to be a poker and various irons in a kettle by the fireplace.

He said, "Can I lean against the chair?"

Denny just looked at him.

"My back, for Christ sake. Can I?"

"Your back? I hope it the hell breaks."

Rick stared at him. "I've got to, I can't—" And then as Denny watched he wriggled over to the chair. He leaned back against it. But he was, he was aware, still far out of reach of the kettle. And still far from him.

Denny slowly looked away again. Rick sat drawing in breaths. He would wait. Maybe Denny would come over, at least come closer. He kept waiting. His fingers felt swollen, were throbbing. He heard Denny yawn, saw him rub his face against his shoulder. He kept watching him, hoping he would fall asleep. But Denny shook himself and straightened up. And looked this way again, briefly.

It had to be now. Before Terri decided to come back.

He sat up a little straighter. Then he let out a soft, "Help me."

Denny looked over at him.

"Help ..."

"Why don't you just fuckin' die, you bastard? Why don't you just die?"

Rick flung his head back. Then staring over at him, and breathing hard, he said with a voice full of scorn, "She's right what she says about you."

Denny stared at him. He started to look away, then looked back. "Who says what about me?" Then when Rick didn't answer, "What'd she say, you bastard?"

Rick still said nothing.

"What's this shit you're givin' me what she said?"

Rick let his head droop forward, but through narrowed eyes he could see Denny rising, could see him approaching slowly. He was only a couple of feet away now. Rick could see his gun, half-lifted.

"What did—"

"Look, I only made it up, I—" and suddenly he was on his feet, one hand lifting the gun wrist, the other closed on Denny's throat, pushing him backward, falling with him, lifting his head by his hair now and slamming it down on the stone floor, lifting and slamming it, lifting and slamming it.

Terri leaped to her feet at the first sound. Holding her gun in both hands, she stood trying to see down the hall through the blackness. Her hands, her legs were trembling.

"Den?"

She walked forward slowly. She reached with one hand into her handbag which she'd grabbed up and flung over her shoulder. She opened it, felt for the bullets. She took out a handful.

"Den?"

She fired twice into that room as she walked.

She wondered should she run out, but where? She didn't even have a key to the car.

She stepped into the doorway, then through it, firing in different directions.

She was breathing hard.

And then suddenly she felt a hand grab her gun hand from behind, and another go over her mouth.

"Just let it go," Rick's voice said. "Let it go. Come on. Let it go."

She fought, she twisted, she writhed from side to side. Then her hand slowly released the gun. And she slumped to her knees, staring down, just breathing, breathing.

*C*HAPTER THIRTY-FIVE

The sirens first, in the distance and now right outside, and then a lot of people were all around her, doing things she didn't see, didn't want to see, because she sat bent over her lap, her eyes tightly closed. The only time she opened her eyes was not when they put on handcuffs but when someone began lifting her up, and she started fighting.

"You don't want to walk in the snow without shoes," a voice said, and she went limp and let them throw something over her, maybe her jacket.

The secret though, she found, was keeping her eyes closed. It helped her mind stay pretty much blank all the way during the ride in the car, and then when they stopped and there were voices all around as they lifted her out, it was like she was in her own private world. And later she found that she didn't even have to close her eyes to keep people out. You could look at them, but though they were there, it didn't matter to you.

One of the first things Rick wanted to know was if anyone in the Devore party—Mr. and Mrs., their daughter and a boyfriend—had been hurt. No. Afterward, always the reporter, the first call he made was to the *Dispatch*, where he spoke to

Joe Cooperman. Cooperman's immediate reaction on hearing his voice was a happy, "Hey," and he took down what
happened. And he told Rick that he'd learned from a "source"
that only a little while ago Mrs. McKenzie had finally admitted that Rick had been interested in finding her daughter and
that she had a gun.

Rick said, "What about that guy they're looking for?"

"Ah, a guy with a grudge but no imagination of his own."

Rick smiled. "I'll see you."

He had other calls to make, fast. Deirdre, his mother, his
uncle.

Late that morning, after retrieving his car from the state
police, he left for home. Terri, who wouldn't even speak up to
confirm her name, would be held in the Poconos, in the
Luzerne County Prison, on charges there before it was determined when she and Denny would be returned on the homi-
cide charges. Denny was in the hospital with a fractured skull.

His answering machine at the apartment was blinking
with messages. Of the eight or nine, two caught his immediate attention. Mr. Devore. And Terri's mother.

He reached Devore first, who had called to thank him for
saving their lives.

Rick said, "I wonder if you could tell me something about
Terri as a little girl."

"God, thinking of that little girl, I can't believe what became of her. And yet when I really think about it, something
of it was there. She'd been such a charming, adventurous little
girl, everything Robin wasn't at that age, which was why I
tried to cultivate their friendship. But I used to worry about
her and had to set down a strong set of rules. If she got it into
her head she wanted to climb a tree or swim out in the middle
of the lake, you'd see her up that tree or way out on the lake."

"Did she ever talk about her mother and father?"

"No, not really that I remember ... Well, this might be interesting. A few days before she was to go home from her first stay in the Poconos she said she wanted to buy some gifts for her mother and father. We took her to a store—they had a lot of Indian-type things—and I remember—I remember even talking about this with my wife—the child had no problem picking out something for her mother, but she couldn't find anything she liked for her father. I mean, she liked a lot of things but it was like he might not like them. Like there was nothing good enough she could give him. I don't know, that's the way I saw it. But it ended up my wife picked out something for her."

Rick finally reached Mary McKenzie about an hour later.

"I'm so sorry," and she began crying, "what I put you through. I'm so sorry. And I'm so happy you're safe. That's all I wanted to tell you."

"Have you seen her yet?"

"They said I can't until tomorrow. I'm going up then, my daughter's taking me. I hired a lawyer there, you know, but he called me, he told me she wouldn't even talk to him."

"You say your daughter ..." He hesitated, then said, "Your husband isn't going?"

"He may go with me, but he says he's not going in. He's afraid he'll only make things worse—like they can *get* worse."

"You haven't asked me, but I think it's important he try to see her."

"Jack," she called to her husband. "I'm talking to Mr. Broder. And he says what I've been saying. You got to go up and see her."

"I'll see her, not now."

"Jack, talk to him. I want you to talk to him."

"Hello," Mr. McKenzie said reluctantly. "Look. I know what'll happen I see her. She'll scream and then I'll start yellin'... Look, we were never close, I don't know why. She was close to her mother, at least she used to be. But she and I— I don't know. I always worked hard, put bread on that table. I—" His voice choked, he began to cry softly. "It's not like I ... ever hit her. I mean, maybe a spank on the behind but I never *hit* her. Did I, Mary?"

"No, I never saw it."

"I never *did* it. Or the other kids. I don't think ever. It's like Mary and I been saying. You have kids and two are okay, and the other one ... And yet you treated 'em all the same. I appreciate what you went through, I appreciate your help, but me goin' up there now, it'll only make it worse."

"I don't want to butt in, Mr. McKenzie, but I would try if I were you. I'd go there. I'd try to let her know I was right there with her."

People, she didn't want no more damn people. She didn't want no more lawyers, she didn't want no more cops, and for sure no psychiatrist. She just wanted them to do whatever they wanted to do with her and get it over with, kill her, send her away forever and throw away the key.

And here there was going to be someone else again.

She was tired of being led here and there from her cell.

But instead of a room where she was all alone with who-ever, she was led into one of those large rooms she used to see in the movies, with cubicles and a guard and where you talked into a phone to a visitor on the other side of a glass.

And as she was led over to a cubicle, she froze.

Not only her mother but Jesus Christ her father!

She started to turn away, but her mother was motioning

frantically to her, and she slowly sat down but didn't pick up the phone. Nor did she look at him. In fact, at first she didn't really look directly at her mother, but slightly to the side, although she could still see her, and her mother never really knew. So she could see her mother with the phone raised to her ear and gesturing for her to pick up the phone. She picked it up. And now her mother's voice saying stupid things like how are you, do they treat you okay. Things you could just answer with a nod.

Then she saw her hand the phone to him, and she wanted to slam hers down. She didn't want any shit! She didn't want his "I told you so's." She didn't want, "What did I tell you, what did I tell you, how many times did I warn you?" But he was saying, and there was a crack in his voice, things like, "We're with you ... do what we can ..."

And though it was hard to look at him, at both of them, she couldn't look away.

The only thing she could do was jump up and run to the doorway because suddenly she was crying and she didn't want them to see her cry.

"Ter!"

It was a wail that almost spun her around. She didn't want to turn ... but she turned. His palms were flat against the glass; he was leaning against it.

"Terri, we'll always be there! We'll be with you! Know it! Know it!"

Tears flooding her eyes, she stared at him, at her. Then she whirled toward the doorway once more.

*C*HAPTER THIRTY-SIX

Joe Cooperman stopped by his office to say, "I hear Denny's going to testify against her."

"I'm hardly surprised. But I don't think he's going to get a deal," Rick said. He was convinced—and it would turn out to be right—that both would get life without parole.

"By the way," Cooperman said with a smile, "you make up your mind yet?"

"Okay, tell me. I give up."

"Going back to being an investigative reporter or stay a columnist to the mind."

Rick smiled back. It wasn't anything that offended him; he'd been thinking it himself. Not about going back to it, but how so much of his mind had been back there. When there was so much here.

He wasn't sure yet what he would do with this story. It would take more than one column—a whole series. Or an article. Or a book—he'd gotten calls from four publishers, including the one he still owed a book to.

What, really, had triggered the whole thing, had set it off with Wyndan's murder? Shrinks who'd never met her had been giving him theories or expounding them to the general media—a boiling of hatred of her father, an act of suppressed love for a father she could never please, disillusionment with the world, the chasm between rich and poor; a combination of several of them, or all, and more.

And why, going back to this, had she let him live? A hostage against the police. That was it, but maybe ... a fragment somewhere ... that her mother liked him ...

He glanced at some notes he'd jotted down.

Go .22, the cheering on.

And then there were her words—"What do you know ..?"

How, whenever he would do it, to begin?

He reached over for a pencil, held it between his hands.

And this wasn't just about those two kids, but him. And a challenge.

What do you know, what the hell do you know, goddamn you, what do you really know?